GAMER SQUAD 3

App of the Living Dead

KIM HARRINGTON

STERLING CHILDREN'S BOOKS
New York

STERLING CHILDREN'S BOOKS
New York

An Imprint of Sterling Publishing Co., Inc.
1166 Avenue of the Americas
New York, NY 10036

ISBN 978-1-4549-2614-6

Distributed in Canada by Sterling Publishing Co., Inc.
c/o Canadian Manda Group, 664 Annette Street
Toronto, Ontario, Canada M6S 2C8
Distributed in the United Kingdom by GMC Distribution Services
Castle Place, 166 High Street, Lewes, East Sussex, England BN7 1XU
Distributed in Australia by NewSouth Books
45 Beach Street, Coogee, NSW 2034, Australia

For information about custom editions, special sales, and premium
and corporate purchases, please contact Sterling Special Sales at
800-805-5489 or specialsales@sterlingpublishing.com.

Manufactured in Canada

Lot #:
2 4 6 8 10 9 7 5 3 1

08/17

sterlingpublishing.com

Design by Ryan Thomann

The first sign that something was wrong was Robbie Martinez projectile-vomiting in science class. We were learning about viruses. And though I didn't think it was barf-worthy, we all have our own threshold for gross. Apparently Robbie's was thinking about a virus invading and reproducing in previously healthy cells. Or so I thought. But when Isaac made the liquid scream in math when we were only talking about ratios, I started to wonder if something else was going on.

"Hey, Bex." My best friend and neighbor, Charlie Tepper, came up to me in the hall with a concerned look. "Why is everyone eating backward today?"

I struggled to pull a book from the pile in my locker without making the rest of them come tumbling out, too. "Must be some kind of stomach bug."

Charlie grimaced. "I remember last year in Runswick a norovirus went around and half their school got it. That's how contagious it can be. They had to close the school for a week and bring in a cleaning crew."

"Gross." I closed my locker door and turned around. My friend Willa Tanaka staggered up to us, clutching her stomach.

"Willa!" I cried. "Are you sick, too?"

She shook her head, and her long black hair flowed from side to side as in one of those slow motion commercials. "I don't have whatever this illness is. But I just watched Mr. Durr upchuck a week's worth of groceries on the whiteboard. So that made me a little woozy."

Yikes. This flu was tearing through school fast. I really didn't want to stick around and risk catching it, but I couldn't just walk out. Maybe I could call my parents and ask them to get me released.

"Bex," a voice called from behind me. "Bex!"

I turned around to see Marcus Moore waving at me from the doorway to the computer lab. My heart sped up. Marcus was the fourth in our little group—Charlie, Willa, Marcus, and I made up the Gamer Squad. Self-titled, but still totally cool. We'd saved the town from video game monsters over summer vacation and an accidental alien invasion in September. My phone was responsible for both disasters, and I still felt a little guilty about that. But it had been a month without drama, and things seemed okay. Mostly because we'd agreed never to play mobile games from Veratrum Games ever again since they'd developed both games that had gone so wrong. In fact, if Veratrum's latest game were called *Flu City* instead of *Zombie Town*, I would have wondered if they were involved with the puke-a-palooza going on right now.

Even though Marcus was one year older, he and I had a lot in common. We were awesome gamers; we both wanted to be programmers; and we both agreed that Speedy's Pizza was far superior to the Wolcott House of Pizza, which was an unpopular opinion in town.

I'd had a crush on Marcus forever. Back in September, my dream came true when he told me he liked me. But now it was October, and we'd never really talked about it since. I'd been hoping that he'd ask me to the Halloween Dance, but he hadn't. At this point, it was only a week away; so my high hopes were currently somewhere in my shoes.

"Bex, c'mere!" Marcus waved excitedly.

Willa poked me in my side. "Go see your lover boy."

Charlie tried to cover a chuckle with his hand.

I rolled my eyes at both of them.

The four of us had been spending a ton of time together since the Gamer Squad formed last month. We hung out in school, played games after school, and talked all night on a group chat. Charlie had been my best friend forever. Willa and I were friends when we were little, then not friends when she dumped me for the popular crowd, then friends again. Now we were closer than ever. And Marcus, . . . well . . .

My stomach did a little *flip-flop* as I walked toward

the computer lab. Was this it? Was Marcus finally asking me to the dance?

I reached the doorway to the lab and put on my best, nonchalant, totally-not-expecting-you-to-ask-me-to-the-dance-and-I'm-actually-really-chill-right-now-and-not-nervous-at-all fake voice. "Hey, Marcus. What's up?"

He motioned for me to come into the room. "I want to show you a game I made."

My heart sank. A computer game? I'd gotten my hopes up—again—and he'd only wanted to talk about games—again. I mean, gaming was my favorite hobby and would hopefully one day be part of my career, but a girl wanted to be asked to a dance now and then, too!

I glanced at the wall clock. "Okay, but I have only three minutes before my next class."

Marcus was beaming with pride, but his fingers were trembling a little. Why was he nervous for me to see his game? Was he worried I wouldn't like it? He led me to the closest computer terminal. His hand hovered over the keyboard.

"Are you ready?" he asked with a giant smile.

As I opened my mouth to say yes, the intercom

clicked on and our principal, Mr. James, began to speak.

"The school is releasing early today due to the—" He paused to let out a moderately gross burp. "Due to the illness affecting many students and staff."

His voice sounded weird. As he tried to begin his next sentence, he gagged and gurgled. I knew what was coming next, but thankfully the intercom clicked off before we all had to listen to it.

Marcus's smile fell.

"That's okay," I said. "You can show me the game tomorrow."

"Sure," he said, nodding, but the disappointment didn't leave his eyes. Whatever this game was, it seemed really important to him.

Charlie poked his head into the room. "Did you hear? Mr. James is letting us out early. My mom already got the emergency autocall and texted that she'll pick us up."

"Okay, cool," I said, reentering the hallway.

With school canceled, kids were rushing out at record speeds but without the usual glee that came along with the early dismissal because of a snowstorm or holiday. They were either sick themselves or trying desperately to leave without touching anything or anyone. And as Andy Badger recycled his lunch on the floor in front of me in a colorful display, only one question went through my head: Why did this have to happen on Taco Tuesday?

The next day, I would have many more questions.

knew it was time for dinner when an amazing smell wafted out of the kitchen and into the living room where I'd been reading. I poked my head in. "Is it ready yet?"

My dad turned around to reveal an apron that said MR. GOOD LOOKIN' IS COOKIN'. He had an abnormally large collection of cheesy aprons. He'd bought one for himself once, and that opened a floodgate for other people to buy him more. My mom, grandparents, neighbors—everyone got him funny aprons, and now it was forever a *thing*. But that was okay because he used them all and he was an amazing cook.

"Just pulling the lasagna out now," he said with the excitement of a kid opening a present.

I set the table and slid into my usual seat as my mom came out of her office. She had her typical flustered look going on—frizzy hair pointing in all directions, glasses on the top of her head, phone two inches from her eyes. She ran her own online personalized jewelry business from our house, which was nice because she was always home but tough because she was never away from work.

"Catching up on email?" I asked as she sat across from me.

She looked up from her phone as if she hadn't even realized I was there. "Oh! Bexley! Um, no emails, just . . ."

Her voice trailed away as her attention returned to her phone. She pounded on the screen with her finger a few times, then flicked. I knew exactly what she was doing.

I crossed my arms. "I thought the rule was no gaming at the table." At least, that had always been the rule—until this month when my parents, of all people, got hooked on a mobile game.

Mom put her phone facedown on the table. "You're right, sweetie." She blew out a breath. "I have a new appreciation for the willpower it must have taken you to stop playing some games. This one really has me."

What my parents *didn't* know was that the main reason I'd quit the two popular games I'd been addicted to was that they'd both unleashed disasters on the town. But, hey, let's go with willpower.

Zombie Town was Veratrum's biggest hit yet. It seemed like everyone in town was hooked, even people who'd never played a game before. But a promise was a promise, and the Gamer Squad had made a pact to never play it. So I wouldn't. No matter how cool it looked. We'd also promised to keep our eyes peeled for video game zombies escaping into the real world, but so far the game seemed normal.

Dad placed the lasagna in the center of the table and served the three of us. But Mom still wasn't ready to move on to food. She lifted her phone up and waved it in my direction. "Are you sure you don't want to try it? It's one of those augmented reality games you like, so the game uses your phone's camera to put the zombies on the real background. You can see a zombie right here in the kitchen!"

I smiled weakly and stabbed my fork into the lasagna. "I know, Mom. But I have another computer game I'm enjoying lately. I don't want to get involved in a new mobile game."

"You know what I love the most about it?" she said, her eyes almost glassy. "It's a zombie game, sure, but it's not violent. You throw *cures* at the zombies to save them. Isn't that wonderful?"

"Yep. I've heard." Boy, had I heard. Every kid at school was talking about it. The teachers. The cafeteria ladies. My favorite librarian. Even our mailman stopped in mid-route to throw a cure at a zombie in our front yard.

Dad looked at me strangely, his fork paused in midair. "I don't get it."

"Don't get what?" I asked.

"You always want to play the latest games and talk about them. This one is so popular. But you don't want to even try it. I think that's weird."

"Yeah," my mom piled on. "Try it. It's just an innocent game."

After you bring a herd of monsters and then an

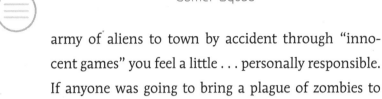

army of aliens to town by accident through "innocent games" you feel a little . . . personally responsible. If anyone was going to bring a plague of zombies to town, it wasn't going to be me. I would not play that game. I wouldn't touch it. I wouldn't even look at it.

I searched my mind for a plausible reason. "It's too popular," I blurted.

"What?" Dad asked, confused.

"I'm sick of playing the same games as everyone else. I'm interested in more obscure games." The classic hipster gamer excuse. Brilliant. If I could have reached around and patted myself on the back without looking suspicious, I would have done it.

But I might have made them suspicious anyway. Both of my parents were suddenly looking at me with strange expressions. I watched as their faces turned a concerning shade of green. Then my mother clapped her hand over her mouth and ran from the table.

"Oh, no!" I said. "Do you have that flu that's going through the school?"

Dad gazed at the cheesy smear of pasta on his plate, and his mouth turned down. "Excuse me," he muttered, then dashed away.

Wonderful. Both my parents were sick. It was only a matter of time before I would have it, too.

I ate my lasagna and cleared off the table. Then I went upstairs to finish my homework. Before bed, I sent off a quick group text.

Everyone still healthy?

Charlie: So far, yeah, but Jason's stream of vomit just contaminated my science experiment.

I giggled, totally able to picture that. Charlie did science experiments in his basement for fun, and this wasn't the first one his older brother Jason had ruined. Jason wanted Charlie to focus on football, but thankfully Charlie wasn't letting his new involvement in sports interfere with his love of science. He'd even incorporated it into an experiment—testing the speed and velocity of footballs inflated to various psi. My best friend was essentially the king of the nerds—and I loved him for it.

The others chimed in quickly after Charlie.

Marcus: I'm good, but my parents both have it.

Willa: My dance class got canceled because Chloe barfed mid-pirouette. She was like a human lawn sprinkler.

I started laughing so hard, my cheeks hurt. I loved my friends. After some rocky starts, the Gamer Squad meant everything to me. We'd been through so much we were practically family.

Meanwhile, my actual family started to ramp it up, taking turns destroying the toilet. My eyes felt heavy, so I shut my phone down for the night and plugged it in to recharge.

I closed my bedroom door rather than fall asleep to the sweet lullaby of my parents ralphing all over the bathroom.

I was surprised when my alarm went off in the morning. I'd thought for sure school would be canceled. But the phone never rang with that beautiful no-school robocall. It must have been one of those quick flus, and enough teachers felt well enough to go to work. Oh, well.

I got dressed in jeans and a white sweater and pulled my giant mess of brown hair up into a ponytail. Yawning, I strolled into the kitchen and got my second surprise. It was empty. In fact, the whole house was eerily quiet.

"Mom? Dad?" I glanced at the time on my phone. Dad was usually in the shower by now. And Mom would be at the kitchen table, eating breakfast and checking her email.

Their bedroom and bathroom had been empty when I walked by to head downstairs. I checked my mom's office, but that, too, was empty. How could my parents be nowhere?

"You guys?" My voice echoed as I approached the front of the house. I heard a low whistling sound, like a rustling breeze. A window in the living room was open, but it was more than that. I walked to the front door and found it ajar. What in the world?

I poked my head outside. My parents were nowhere in sight. This made no sense. I marched back into the kitchen to see if they'd left me a note, then stopped, squinting my eyes.

The little whiteboard where we left messages for each other had only one word: *RUN*.

3

It wasn't the first time my parents had gone for a morning run before work, but I thought it was a little weird. I mean, they'd been *so* sick. They definitely weren't thinking clearly, yet one of them had left the front door open, and the message on the whiteboard was clearly hastily written. But they were finally out of the bathroom, and it seemed like they were feeling better, so I was glad about that. It must have been one of those stomach bugs that comes on fast and strong but leaves quickly. Which was why school hadn't been canceled. Boo.

With a groan, I slung my backpack over my shoulder and headed outside to meet Charlie. We walked to school together every morning. I hoped he hadn't gotten sick overnight.

I righted a fallen Halloween decoration—my yard was full of them. Wolcott got kind of competitive around Halloween. People wanted to be known for giving good candy or for their house having cool decorations. But what had started several years ago with a few houses stringing up orange lights and fake ghosts had turned into a competition. My parents had been sucked in, too, and our front yard was riddled with witches, tombstones, and giant plastic spiders.

I stopped at the sidewalk. A perfect circle of puke lay on the walk in front of my house. I raised my eyebrows. Strange. It mustn't have been from my parents, though. They wouldn't have gone for a run if they were still sick. I shrugged and made my way to Charlie's.

He came out of his house at full speed, zipping up a gray sweatshirt and running his fingers through his messy blond hair.

"Sorry I'm late!" he said, running toward me. "My mom usually wakes me up but no one's home.

They were up half the night with Jason, so they probably took him to our doctor."

"You mean you weren't by his side taking care of
him?" I joked.

Charlie gagged. "I want no part of his germs. I must
have washed my hands a hundred times last night."

I laughed and found a pebble to kick. Charlie and
I played this game on the way to school where we
took turns kicking a pebble the whole way. It wasn't
superfun or anything, but it was tradition.

After a few blocks, I started to notice something—
or, rather, the lack of something. Not one car had
passed us. It was early in the morning, sure, but we
usually saw a few cars on our way to school. And
where were the buses? We hadn't seen one of those
yet, either.

A chill crept down my back. This was weird.

Charlie must have realized it, too. He glanced
nervously over his shoulder. "Lots of people staying
home sick today, I guess."

"Yeah." It was the only thing that made sense.
The flu had descended on the town overnight. Everyone was stuck at home.

Still, it was eerie to approach the school and find

the parking lot mostly empty. A couple of kids shuffled around slowly. One eighth grader I recognized took one look at the school, turned around on his heel, and walked away.

Marcus and Willa were waiting for us at the entrance, even though we usually met inside.

"You guys," Marcus said as we neared them. "It's a ghost town in there. I thought I saw Mr. Durr going around a corner but no one else."

"Then why didn't they cancel school?" Charlie asked.

"Think about who sends out the emergency autocall," Willa said. "The principal, right? And we know for sure he has the flu, since he nearly barfed midintercom message yesterday."

Huh. Could Mr. James be too sick to even send a phone message? This wasn't like any other flu I'd ever seen.

My eyes scanned the parking lot. I recognized Robbie ahead, moving away from the school, but he seemed to be walking strangely. He was the quarterback of the middle school football team, and Charlie was his backup. I wondered if something had happened to him.

"Did Robbie get injured?" I motioned with my chin and everyone turned to look.

Charlie shrugged. "Not that I know of. But he does look . . . off."

"Hey, Robbie!" I called.

He turned around slowly and shuffled toward us, dragging his feet more than walking. His head lilted to the side at an uncomfortable angle, like he didn't have the muscle control to hold it up. The flu must have really wiped him out. I wondered why he hadn't stayed home to rest.

He got closer but still didn't say anything.

Willa stepped up to him. "Did you barf up your brain or something?"

Robbie lifted his head. I could have sworn he had dark brown eyes, but right now they were a strange light gray color. A prickly feeling crawled over my skin.

Willa snapped her fingers in front of his face. "Hello? What is with you?"

"Willa," I began, my voice wary. "I think—"

Robbie's mouth opened, and he flashed his teeth.

"What the heck?" Willa screeched, backing away.

Then he charged.

The four of us ran toward the school, with Robbie lumbering closely behind. I mentally willed myself not to trip and fall like one of those people in horror movies, as if telling myself not to trip would actually make me not trip. Marcus pulled open the front door and we piled inside, closing it quickly behind us. I exhaled loudly. We all made it.

But Robbie was still advancing.

"We need to lock the doors!" I yelled.

Charlie examined the entrance. "I can't. We need a key to lock it."

Robbie was almost here. Only a few steps away.

"We can use a broom from the janitor's closet," Willa said. "Pull it through the handles and it will keep the door closed."

"There's no time!" Marcus cried. "He's here! Everyone help me keep the door closed."

We all grasped the large silver handles and pulled. I hoped that whatever had happened to Robbie hadn't given him superstrength. He was right outside the door now, close enough that I could see his weirdly gray eyes through the window. But he didn't

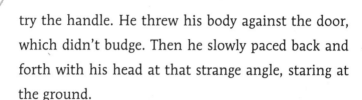

try the handle. He threw his body against the door, which didn't budge. Then he slowly paced back and forth with his head at that strange angle, staring at the ground.

"I don't think he knows how to open the door," Charlie said after a few moments.

We cautiously let go of the handles and stepped back. I let out a relieved breath, but it wasn't like our problem was solved. Robbie was still right outside the door, waiting for us.

"What *was* that?" My voice shook even though I was trying my best to stay calm.

"That was our quarterback," Willa said, matter-of-factly.

"You know what I mean." I shoved my trembling hands into the pockets of my jeans. "Is Robbie a—a . . ."

"Zombie?" Marcus said.

I closed my eyes. "I don't even want to hear that word."

"I'm going to get a broom from the janitor's closet," Willa said. "Then we can be sure this door will stay closed."

"I'll go with you," Marcus offered.

Charlie and I stood in the hallway alone. He looked at me warily. "It's happening again, isn't it?"

"Yep."

"It's worse this time."

"The worst," I agreed.

4

he broom handle trick worked perfectly. Robbie seemed content to pace back and forth by the door, waiting to eat our brains— or at least, I assumed that's what he wanted to do. So maybe we could safely find another way out.

"We could go out the back entrance," Charlie suggested. "And then cut through the woods. That way we avoid the parking lot—and Robbie—entirely."

"Sounds like a good plan," I said, and Marcus nodded in agreement.

Willa chewed on her thumbnail. "But what if Robbie's not the only one? What if there are more of . . . *them* inside here with us?"

Charlie scratched his head. "We'll just have to be careful."

We crept down the hall, elbow to elbow. The school didn't look particularly sinister. It was daytime, for one thing, and all the lights were on. But walking by one empty classroom after another gave me the creeps.

A shuffling sound stopped us in our tracks. We neared the end of the hall, with only one room left—Ms. Happel's English classroom. We all glanced around, searching one another's faces for what to do. The sound continued and the lights went off in the classroom. A shadow cast its darkness across the doorway.

And Ms. Happel came out.

A totally human Ms. Happel.

She gasped, hand on her heart, as she saw us. Admittedly, we probably looked kind of creepy, standing completely still all in a row like that.

"Students! What are you doing?" She had her coat thrown over one arm, like she was on her way out, and she wore one of her many cat sweaters. Yes, many. This one had a cat's face with sequins for eyes.

"We're heading out the back way," I said. "Another student is by the front door, acting strangely."

She nodded somberly. "We have to move quickly. I've been watching out the window. There are several people acting . . . strangely. This flu seems to have a unique effect on them."

That was one way to put it.

She closed her classroom door. "Let's get out of here. Follow me."

I had to admit, I felt a little better knowing an adult was now in charge. I'd tried calling my parents on their cell phones several times already but neither one had answered. I didn't want to think about what that could mean. At least now Ms. Happel would take care of us.

We turned the corner, following our teacher closely, until she stopped short.

Farther down the hall stood Mr. Durr, my science teacher. He was standing still, sort of staring at a locker.

"Mr. Durr?" Ms. Happel called. "We're heading out. Would you like to come with us?"

His head twisted toward the sound of her voice, and he started walking. It was the same shuffle-drag-shuffle that Robbie had done outside.

"Oh, no," Charlie said.

The science teacher tilted his head to the side and a long string of drool leaked from his open mouth.

"He's one of them!" Marcus yelled.

Before we could get away, Mr. Durr had reached Ms. Happel and grabbed her arm. She gasped and tried to pull it back, but he clamped down on it with his teeth.

The floor seemed to move underneath me. One of my teachers had just *bit* another. I couldn't believe this was happening. My brain was screaming things like, *Run, dummy!* but my feet seemed glued to the floor.

Marcus, however, sprang into action. Letting out a roar, he slipped his backpack off his shoulder and swung it like a two-ton weapon at Mr. Durr's head. To be fair, that thing was full of books and a laptop, so it was pretty heavy. And Mr. Durr went down—hard.

"Come on, Ms. Happel," Willa said, pulling at her unbitten arm. "Let's go!"

27

But the teacher stayed put, swaying in her spot.

"She must be in shock," I said.

"Ms. Happel!" Charlie yelled. "We don't know how long he'll be down for. He's going to get back up. We have to go!"

She blinked heavily, as if awakening from a deep slumber, and slowly turned her head to face us. Her dark eyes lightened until they were a pale, shimmering gray.

I stumbled backward, my hands reaching out to grab on to my friends.

"Is she—is she?" Marcus stammered.

As if in response, our sweet English teacher growled and snapped at the air.

"Run!" Charlie yelled.

We dashed into the nearest open classroom, slamming the door closed behind us. Ms. Happel pressed her forehead against the small glass window, but didn't try the knob. Mr. Durr soon joined her. He had a small lump on his forehead from Marcus's bag.

"We're safe," I said. "They can't open doors."

"Yeah, but we can't stay in here forever," Charlie said through ragged breaths.

"It's the game," Marcus said, pacing back and forth. "*Zombie Town*. It turned people into actual zombies."

Willa slammed her hand on a desk, startling me. "So who did it?" she yelled. "Who broke our pact and played the game? Who set off this disaster?"

Marcus quickly shook his head.

"I didn't," Charlie and I said simultaneously, stumbling over each other's words.

"Someone did this!" Willa screeched. "We made a promise to never play a Veratrum game again, but one of us did."

I knew I hadn't played. And I knew Charlie hadn't played. Marcus seemed too busy lately creating that new game in the computer lab. And Willa had clearly kept her promise.

"I don't think any of us played," I said.

"That's it," Charlie said, slowly raising his eyes from the floor.

I turned to look at him. "What?"

"We haven't really stopped to think about why we're *not* zombies," he said. "What do we have in common?"

It dawned on me instantly. "We *didn't* play."

Charlie nodded. "Everyone I know who got sick had played the game. Jason. Robbie. Even Mr. Durr talked about the game in class."

"You're right," Willa said. "Chloe was addicted, and she was the first to puke in ballet class."

"Both my parents played and they got sick last night," Marcus said. "They were locked in their room this morning. I assumed they were sleeping. Does this mean that they're zombies?"

I swallowed hard. That would mean my parents were zombies, too. "I think so," I said sadly. Then I pushed the thought to the back of my mind.

"But it's not just the people who played the game we should be worried about," Charlie said. "The people who didn't play aren't safe either because they can become a zombie if they're bitten. Mr. Durr just turned Ms. Happel!"

"No one is safe," I croaked.

Marcus started pacing again. "We have to get out of here."

"What can we use as weapons?" Willa asked.

Charlie tapped on his chin. "Do they have real knives in the cafeteria or only the plastic ones they give us?"

"They must have real knives for chopping and meal prep," Marcus said.

"You guys!" I cried. "We are not going to stab anyone!"

"Then how are we going to get out of here?" Willa asked.

"We have to defend ourselves," Charlie said.

Marcus moved closer to me. "Mr. Durr bit Ms. Happel and turned her into a zombie. You saw it."

"There has to be another way." I shook my head. "I know you're focused on the whole zombie thing, but deep down, they're still our teachers. And Robbie is still Robbie." I took a deep breath. "If we came across my parents in the parking lot, would you hurt them, too?"

They all stared at one another and then at the floor. I didn't want to know the answer.

"I'm calling 911," Willa said.

We waited as she made the call. Scowling, she hung up and tried again. And again.

"What's going on?" Charlie asked.

"Busy signal," she said gravely. "Every time."

Thoughts swirled in my head. We'd figured out that zombies couldn't open doors. But then how did my parents get out of the house? I thought about the messily written message on the whiteboard and the answer came to me. One of them transformed first. The other wrote the warning to me and lured the zombie out of the house before turning, too. All to keep me safe. And it had worked.

My head snapped up. "I have an idea."

Willa, Charlie, and Marcus circled around me.

"We know they can't open doors, right? So we use that to our advantage." I pointed at the side door. It didn't lead to the hallway where our teachers stood waiting to devour us. It led to the classroom next door.

I continued, "Almost all the classrooms have connecting doors to the classroom beside it. We go from room to room, avoiding the hall. And when we've gone as far as we can, we run for it."

My friends all looked at me, picturing it in their heads.

"It's as good a plan as any," Charlie said.

Marcus nodded. "Let's do it."

Willa grabbed a ruler from the teacher's desk. Charlie raised his eyebrows at her, but she only clutched it more tightly.

"Hey, it's better than no weapon at all."

5

Marcus inched open the door that led into the next classroom. He poked his head in, then audibly exhaled. "It's empty."

We all piled into the room—from the algebraic equation on the board, a math room—and closed the door. This was a good plan, I told myself. Use the inter-classroom doors to avoid the hallway. And when we got as far as we could, we'd make a run for it to the nearest exit.

The only thing that could ruin this plan was if a zombie was actually *in* one of the classrooms. Which I was sure we were all thinking about, since the others looked as nervous as a bunch of gazelles in lion territory.

Charlie looked at the numbers on the board. "Why did the bacteria fail the math test?"

"What?" Marcus asked.

"He tells science jokes when he gets nervous," I whispered.

"Oh," Marcus said. "Um, okay. Why did the bacteria fail the math test?"

Charlie answered, "They thought multiplication was the same as division."

No one laughed.

"Get it?" he said. "Because bacteria cells divide and—"

"Yeah, we get it," Willa cut in. "It's just not the best time right now, Charlie."

Frowning, Charlie put his ear against the door to the next classroom. "Sounds empty."

He outstretched one trembling hand toward the knob.

Willa reached out and grabbed his other hand. Charlie's eyes widened, and he looked down at her clasped fingers like they were some strange foreign object he'd never seen before. But he held on tightly.

I'd been starting to suspect that Willa had a crush on Charlie. And I hadn't yet decided how I felt about it. But now wasn't the time to explore those feelings. Plus, Willa holding his hand seemed to be useful, because Charlie was suddenly more confident. His shoulders squared, and he flung open the door.

The classroom was dark but quiet. Charlie and Willa crept inside. Marcus and I followed, running our hands along the wall looking for the light switch. I found it and flicked it on, just as something made a huge crash.

My eyes adjusted to the light. It was a social studies room, as evidenced by the globe Charlie had knocked to the floor. And it seemed they had plans to watch a movie today. The shades were drawn and the projector was set up and ready to go. The door to the hallway was cracked open just an inch, but Marcus rushed to close it before any zombies could sneak in and join us.

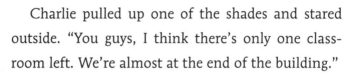

Charlie pulled up one of the shades and stared outside. "You guys, I think there's only one classroom left. We're almost at the end of the building."

Willa took an elastic out of her pocket and pulled her hair up into a tight bun. "The next room is my health class. If that room is empty, too, *and* we can be quiet,"—she cut her eyes to Charlie and the globe he'd crashed into, "then it will be clear sailing. There's an exit in the hall right outside that classroom."

I took a deep breath. "I'll go first this time." Both Marcus and Charlie had taken turns leading the way. It was only fair. Terrifying, but fair.

I leaned my ear up against the door like they had done, but all I could hear was my own heart pounding loudly in my chest . . . and in my ears and my throat. I mean, was my heart traveling throughout my body? Did I suddenly have several hearts?

No more procrastinating, I told myself. *Just do it*. The room would be empty, like the others. I'd gotten myself so worked up that my hand was sweaty and slick. It took me a couple of tries to turn the knob, then I let the door sway inward.

Willa was right; it was the health room. There was an illustration of a uterus on the board, which I didn't really need to see at that moment, and posters reminding us to eat our vegetables and to exercise. No lights were on, but the shades were up, giving the room a dim yellow glow. The coast seemed to be clear, so I inched inside. The only other place left to look was behind the door, so I poked my head around it . . . and screamed.

I fell backward onto my butt in the middle of the room. The boys rushed in after me, with Willa close behind, holding her ruler over her shoulder like a baseball bat. But then they started laughing. Like, doubled-over, can't catch your breath laughing. And I realized what I had done.

I'd screamed at a fake skeleton.

"That's Fred," Willa said between gasps of laughter. "He's made of plastic."

And I could see that now. "Fred" was a fake skeleton used for health class instruction. He even had a metal pole and stand keeping him upright.

"Okay, okay," I said. "You guys can stop laughing at me now."

"But," Charlie choked out, "you should have seen your face. You fell down!"

Marcus was backing toward the hall door, still laughing. "You screamed so loud! It was hilarious."

37

Every cell in my body froze. The door to the hall was open. Just a crack, but open. And we'd been so loud. We could have certainly attracted some zombie attention.

I held a hand up. "Marcus! The door!"

But as soon as the words left my mouth, Ms. Happel lumbered through it and chomped her teeth down on Marcus's shoulder.

He cried out in pain, his eyes widening in shock and then realization. He knew he was done for. He'd turn into a zombie any moment now. And he'd bite us next.

So he pushed Ms. Happel out into the hall and followed her. And with one last glance back at us, he closed the classroom door, saving us from what he was about to become.

6

found it hard to breathe. It was such a natural thing—breathing—I'd done it without even trying since the second I was born. But I seemed to have forgotten how. I pressed my hand on my chest, pushing as if my lungs had a reset button. But the only thing that came out was a high-pitched noise.

"Bex?" Charlie's face swam into my vision. "Look at me, Bex."

"Marcus," I said between heavy breaths. "Zombie."

"Yes," Charlie said sadly. "He is."

I scurried over to the small window in the door. Ms. Happel loomed on the other side, her jaw hanging low, her cat sweater twinkling. Beyond her was that exit door we'd needed so badly. And beside her was Marcus. His hazel eyes, which I'd always found so dreamy, were now a deadly gray.

I squeezed my eyes shut. Nope. This wasn't happening. But when I reopened them, Marcus was still a zombie. Tip: Denial does not work.

Tears streamed down my cheeks. So I had my first kinda, sorta, maybe, could-be boyfriend, and he turned into a zombie. Story of my life. I clenched my fists as the shock wore off and morphed into anger.

"How is this happening?" I yelled. "*Another* disaster in our town. Another time everyone around me is in danger."

"You are *really* not a lucky person," Willa said.

"Thanks for pointing that out," I snapped. "It's appreciated."

"You know those people who win the lottery multiple times?" she said. "You're like them, except in a bad way."

I started to pace, pulling my hands through my hair.

"How can you joke around at a time like this?" Charlie asked Willa. "Marcus is a zombie. And it's not Bex's fault—she didn't even play the game—but our friend is gone forever."

She shrugged. "I don't think he is."

I stopped pacing and stared at her.

"Hear me out," she said. "This was caused by the *Zombie Town* game, right?"

Charlie shrugged. "We're assuming."

"And what was the object of the game? I'm sure you heard people talking about it."

I wiped tears off my cheek with the sleeve of my sweater. "To cure the zombies."

"Right. So maybe . . ."

"We can cure him with the game." I stopped sniffling as hope rose in my chest.

But Charlie was still frowning. "I don't know," he said. "The *Alien Invasion* game didn't work on real, live aliens. What if *Zombie Town* doesn't work on real zombies?"

Willa glanced down at the floor, silent.

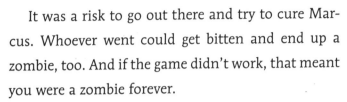

It was a risk to go out there and try to cure Marcus. Whoever went could get bitten and end up a zombie, too. And if the game didn't work, that meant you were a zombie forever.

But I felt like this was my fault. I told everyone not to get weapons. It was my idea to go through the classrooms. It was my scream that had caused everyone to laugh and attract the zombie into the room. And even though I couldn't think of any reason why, I felt responsible for the game affecting the real world. After all, it was my monsters that had escaped from *Monsters Unleashed*. It was my phone that had summoned aliens to town from *Alien Invasion*. This was my fault, too. Somehow. Probably.

I lifted my chin. "I'll do it. I'll play the game and try to cure Marcus."

Charlie dashed over to my side. "That's not a good idea, Bex. Let's just wait it out. We'll keep trying phone numbers until someone answers. Maybe someone will come get us."

"I don't want to wait," I said.

"But what if the game turns you into a zombie, too?" Charlie asked. "All the other players turned."

"We don't know if that would happen, though," I said. "Maybe you have to play for a really long time."

Willa spoke up. "I don't think so."

"Why not?" Charlie asked.

"Think about it. People have been playing this game for weeks, right? Some people played it a little bit here and there, some people played it for hours on end, but *everyone* got sick and then turned into a zombie on the *same* day. If the game continuously turned people into zombies after playing it for a certain amount of time, people would have changed on different days. Not all at once. It's like . . . a switch flipped."

My hands curled into fists. "Veratrum did something."

Willa nodded. "That's my theory."

"So if that's right, then the switch—or code, or whatever—already happened and I won't turn into a zombie if I play the game now," I said.

"But we can't know that for sure!" Charlie insisted.

I took a deep breath. "It's worth the risk to save Marcus. This is my responsibility. I'll do it."

I slid my phone out of my pocket, went to the

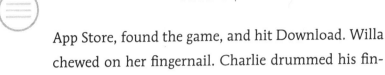
App Store, found the game, and hit Download. Willa chewed on her fingernail. Charlie drummed his fingers on the teacher's desk.

"Okay, it's installed," I said.

Charlie peered over my shoulder, "I watched my brother play. Its functionality is just like *Monsters Unleashed*. You toss the cure at a zombie. A direct hit to the face works best. If you hit an arm or shoulder, it may bounce off. Oh, and the zombies can deflect. So you need to be quick and accurate."

"And the cure is all for fictional, video game zombies," Willa reminded me. "We have no idea how the game will work on real zombies."

"If it even will," Charlie added. "Are you sure about this?"

My eyes went to the window again. Marcus was shuffling back and forth in front of the exit, his head at an unnatural angle. I *had* to try.

"Yeah, I'm sure."

I opened the game. The *Zombie Town* logo took over the screen. It included a cowering girl and a gory-looking zombie looming over her. Creepy horror music came out of the phone's speaker.

"That's reassuring," I said.

Willa put her hands on my shoulders and forced me to look her in the eye. "It's a game. Like all the other games you've played. You're the best gamer I know. You've got this."

I was glad she was confident because my legs suddenly felt as stable as cooked spaghetti.

"Close the door behind me as fast as possible," I said. "If anything happens to me, just stay in here."

Willa nodded, her mouth tight. I could tell she was trying not to look scared so I wouldn't feel scared. Charlie wouldn't even look at me. His eyes focused on a desk in the corner, and they were glistening like they were just about to fill with tears.

"I'll be fine," I said. "I'm sure Willa is right. The point of the game is to cure the zombies. This will work."

I snuck up to the door as quietly as possible and peeked through the window. Ms. Happel had moved on down the hall, her shuffling frame only a shadow in the distance. But Marcus was still here. He seemed to be lumbering around in a mindless circle, even bumping into the wall now and then. My heart cinched. Marcus had such a brilliant mind. Was it still in there somewhere? Would he come back to us?

With one last deep breath, I glanced down at the phone. It was ready, locked, and loaded. I turned the handle of the door and crept out into the hall.

Charlie and Willa closed the door behind me. I could feel their eyes on my back, watching me with their hearts in their throat. But I felt strangely, suddenly calm.

Marcus hadn't heard or seen me yet. I aimed the phone until his back was in the center of the target. Then I used my finger to swipe up and launch a cure.

On the screen, the "cures" were little science beakers. I wasn't expecting that actual lab equipment would pop out of my phone and hit Marcus in the head. I didn't know what I was expecting. But something happened: A ray of light came from my phone, where the flashlight beam comes from. But it was bright red, like a laser, and it hit Marcus's right shoulder.

And he moved.

He'd been *actually* hit by something. Some force of light. And he was really, really, unhappy about it. He twisted around, baring his teeth, and growling. His hungry eyes lit up when they saw me.

And not in the way you want your crush's eyes to light up when he sees you.

I launched another cure. This one hit him in the leg. He stumbled a bit but kept advancing—and certainly wasn't cured. I aimed again and tossed one that seemed to be heading in the right direction but—being a zombie—he staggered a step and it glanced off his arm.

The game *was* doing something in the real world—making a zombie mad! Even more mad than, you know, usual zombie rage. Marcus was so close now. I could run, but Ms. Happel was down that hall somewhere. I had to stand my ground and keep trying.

It would have been easier if this wasn't my *first* time playing the game. Stupid pact!

I took a deep breath, aimed the phone, and focused. *Right in the head. Square in that handsome face.* My finger swiped. The red ray of light streamed out of my phone . . . and got him right in the forehead.

He stood completely still, stunned. Then, as I watched, his eyes turned from that strange gray back to hazel. He blinked slowly, coming out of his zombie state.

"It worked, guys," I whispered, waving my hand. "It's safe to come out." I wanted to yell and cheer, but we needed to be quiet. We didn't want to catch the attention of Ms. Happel or Mr. Durr again.

Charlie and Willa poked their heads out of the door, then tiptoed out.

"It really worked?" Charlie asked hesitantly. "He's not a zombie?"

Just then, Marcus raised his hands, curled them into claws, and groaned, "Brainssssss . . ."

Willa gasped. Charlie put his fists up like he was going to box three rounds with the zombie. But Marcus, rather than lunging for our brains, bent over at the waist, laughing uncontrollably.

"You guys are so gullible," he said.

Willa punched him in the arm. "That wasn't funny!"

"Yeah," I said. "We were really worried that the cure didn't work and that you'd be stuck like that forever."

"Wait," he said, confusion falling over his face. "Stuck like what?" He glanced around, like he just realized where he was. "What am I doing here?"

"What's the last thing you remember?" Charlie asked.

Marcus yawned as he thought for a moment. "I walked to school this morning. No one was here because everyone was sick with that flu. And now I'm here with you guys."

"You don't remember zombie Robbie?" Willa asked in disbelief. "And zombie Mr. Durr? And zombie Ms. Happel biting your shoulder?"

He reached a hand up and squeezed. "My shoulder *does* hurt." He started to sway in place. "Wow, you guys. I'm really tired."

And then he collapsed to the floor.

dropped to my knees and leaned over Marcus. "Are you okay?"

His eyes fluttered. He hadn't lost consciousness, but he seemed about to. Something wasn't right.

He sat up, blinking slowly at all of us. "I'm really tired, guys. And I feel super-weak. All I want to do is go to bed."

Charlie carefully helped him to his feet. "Okay, but we have to get out of the school first. It's not safe. There are zombies in here."

Marcus scrunched up his nose. "You keep saying that, but I'm having a hard time believing it."

Willa sighed. "Everyone who played *Zombie Town* got sick yesterday. And today they're actual zombies. But also, if they bite someone, that person turns into a zombie, too. Like you did after Ms. Happel bit you. So no one is safe."

"But we can cure them with the game," I added, "like I cured you."

Marcus looked at me, and I could tell his mind was slowly putting it all together. "How did you know that it would work for sure?"

I shrugged.

"You risked your life to try to cure me?" he asked, eyes wide.

I stared down at my shoes as I felt my cheeks turn bright red. "Uh—"

Smooth, Bex. Real smooth.

"Yes, she did," Willa piped up. "She was the only one brave enough to try it."

Marcus's drained face broke out into a grin. "Thanks, Bex."

"You're welcome," I said and grinned back.

"Let me look at your wound," Charlie said, pulling

Marcus's clothing off his shoulder a bit. "It doesn't look too bad."

Willa rose up on her tiptoes and took a look. "My little brothers bite me harder than that, and they're human."

"So I don't have an oozing, zombie-infected wound. That's good." Marcus swayed a little. "I still need to lie down, though."

"We have to get him somewhere safe," I said.

"My house . . . is not safe," Marcus slurred. "Both parents played the game."

"No one was home at my house this morning," Charlie said. "I'd assumed my parents had taken Jason to our doctor." His voice caught a bit. "But now it seems more likely that Jason bit them while I was sleeping, and they ran out of the house while they could still open doors. At least that means the house is a safe spot. I could bring him there."

"Okay," Willa said. "But I think Bex and I should head somewhere else."

I furrowed my brow. "Where?"

"We have to go to the police this time. No one is picking up at 911, but maybe there are still some officers at the station."

We didn't go to the police during the summer's monster problem because only people who'd played *Monsters Unleashed* could see the monsters, and we knew the police wouldn't believe us. And I hadn't wanted to involve any authorities with the previous month's alien invasion because I only wanted to send the aliens home, not get them captured. But Willa was right—this time we were in over our heads. Enough people had played the game to fill the town with zombies. And if they could spread the zombie infection with a bite, the whole town would soon be overcome. We had to get help. And fast.

"You're right," I said. "But I don't like the idea of splitting up."

"It'll be okay," Charlie said. "Let's text each other every few minutes for updates."

I shook my head. It felt strange to split up and go our separate ways. "Isn't this what dumb people do in horror movies before they get killed?"

Willa snorted. "When did you become Queen Pessimist of Negative Land?"

"Since monsters from my phone escaped into the real world, and then I went on a field trip and summoned aliens to town, and then—"

Willa held a hand up. "Okay, okay. I get it. But you're just unlucky. None of that was your fault."

"It was my phone both times!"

"You were playing a game," Charlie said. "It's got to be Veratrum's fault. For however they developed these games. They're not normal."

"Charlie's right," Marcus said. "You saw that line of code in *Alien Invasion*. It was like nothing we'd ever seen before—it was a new programming language! Veratrum did this. Maybe even on purpose."

Veratrum *was* totally shady. And they'd even sent someone to follow us in a fake plumbing van, which wasn't something a normal game developer did to its best customers. I'd thought they were just watching us because we had messed up their games, but maybe they were watching us because they thought we'd caught on to what they were doing. There was something bad going on at Veratrum. But I still felt responsible. I couldn't shake it.

Marcus came closer and said in a low voice, "You need to look at the whole picture. Not one part of it. Remember that."

I nodded and agreed, mainly to get everyone to stop talking. I knew they were only being good friends and trying to make me feel better, but part of me didn't *want* to feel better. I knew that wasn't healthy, but I had bigger things on my plate at the moment.

"Fine," I agreed. "We'll split up."

We made it out the back exit and successfully avoided the handful of zombies staggering through the parking lot. If Marcus didn't believe us at first, he definitely believed us now. We'd become a *real* zombie town.

And as Charlie and Marcus took a left at the end of the road and Willa and I took a right, I gave one last glance over my shoulder. Charlie held Marcus's arm across his shoulders, keeping him upright as they chugged along.

I knew this made the most sense. We had to go to the police station and get help. And Marcus was almost asleep on his feet. He'd only slow us down and get us all eaten. This was the right decision.

But my stomach still felt like I'd chugged a full glass of sour milk.

The walk downtown was weird. No cars drove past. No one was hustling and bustling in and out of the little stores. It was like a ghost town.

As we neared Bodhi's Diner, my stomach grumbled. It was well past lunchtime, and I hadn't eaten since breakfast. But we didn't exactly have time to stop for a stack of pancakes. Still, I looked longingly in the big front window as we approached.

A pair of hands slammed against the glass.

Willa and I jumped back, grabbing each other. Mr. and Mrs. Patel, the owners of the diner, pressed their faces against the glass, mouths open. I thought about my friend Vanya, their daughter. She wasn't a gamer and had told me once that she thought her parents were "wasting their time" playing *Zombie Town* so much. And now they were actual zombies. If Vanya had been in the diner before school this morning, she had probably turned, too. Zombie customers joined the Patels—hands and bodies slamming at the glass, jaws opening and closing. I searched the faces, but I couldn't find Vanya.

They slammed on the glass again, harder this time.

"Let's go," Willa said, her voice tight. "I don't know how strong that glass is."

She was right. Plus, there was nothing we could do. We couldn't bust into the restaurant and cure them all without getting bitten ourselves. And we didn't even know if the cure worked. Marcus was definitely still *off*. We couldn't handle this ourselves. We needed the police.

"Here we are," Willa said a few minutes later.

The old police station was short and squat and looked like a gray concrete Lego. I don't know what I expected. Sirens? People running in and out? Instead, it looked deadly quiet.

My shoulders sagged. I had a bad feeling about this. "Let's head in."

As soon as we walked through the front door, I knew things were not good. Mostly because the dispatcher was a zombie. But I'm good like that with obvious clues.

She had a big poof of pale blonde hair piled high on her head and wore a zip-up Wolcott fleece jacket. She leaned forward, jaws snapping at the air, but for some reason she wasn't lunging out of her seat and charging at us.

"Look," Willa said, pointing down. "Someone handcuffed her to the leg of the desk."

Thank you, brave soul. Now that I didn't have to worry about her eating my face, I could take a look around. She had a couple of phones on her desk, both off the hook, with multiple lines that were all blinking red. That was why the calls to 911 weren't getting through—there was no human here to answer them.

Chairs and papers were strewn about. Shards from a smashed coffeepot were scattered over the floor.

"Looks like there was a struggle," I said, "and everyone took off."

"Not everyone." Willa motioned to the back of the room where a zombie police officer lay on the floor, writhing but unable to do much more because he was also handcuffed to his desk leg.

Willa raised her eyebrows, impressed. "Someone was smart and brave enough to handcuff these two zombies before taking off."

"Too bad everyone in town couldn't be hand-cuffed to something," I muttered.

The groaning zombie on the floor had a bunch of foamy spittle in his mustache that was majorly grossing me out, so I searched the room for clues. Either there had been a chair-throwing competi-tion or a few police officers turned into zombies and scared the others off.

I stopped at a desk with a nameplate that said Detective Palamidis. His or her appointment calen-dar was open on the computer and one word caught my eye. *Veratrum.*

3:00 P.M. Veratrum emp—whistleblower?

"Hey, Willa. Check this out. This detective was supposed to meet a Veratrum employee today." I read over the entry again. "What's a whistleblower?" I pictured someone whose job was to walk around the office dressed like a gym teacher and blow a whistle to keep people awake in their cubicles.

Willa squinted at the screen. "I saw a documentary on that once. Whistleblowers are employees who find out something bad about their company and go to the authorities."

My heart sped up a bit. "So someone was going to tell on Veratrum today?"

"Yeah, but tell what?"

That Veratrum had plans to zombify the whole town? Would they have really done that on purpose? And why? Whatever the whistleblower had to say, it seemed to be too late. Veratrum had gone so far this time, Wolcott might never be saved.

Mustache Zombie made a gross, guttural sound. I felt bad for him, rolling around on the floor like that, his arm connected to the desk. He looked like a living nightmare right now but underneath he was a human being. Maybe even a human with information about this so-called whistleblower meeting.

"Should we play the game and cure the two of them?" I asked.

Willa looked unsure. "We don't know what's wrong with Marcus."

I shrugged. "It can't be any worse than zombie-ism."

"True. And if it doesn't work, they'll still won't be a risk. If zombies can't open doors, they certainly can't unlock handcuffs."

I pointed. "I'll take mustache man and you cure the dispatcher. You'll have to install the game first."

She frowned. "But I'm not allowed to download large files unless I'm on Wi-Fi."

"I think your parents will forgive you for going over your data cap this month with the zombie apocalypse and all."

"You don't know how strongly my parents feel about our data cap."

I threw my hands up. "Just download it already!"

Willa installed the game and walked back to the dispatcher while I focused on Mustache Zombie. I clicked on *Zombie Town* and waited for the creepy opening logo and music to pass. Then I aimed my sights.

"Ready to be cured?" I asked.

Mustache Zombie growled in response.

It was much easier when the zombie was trapped on the floor and I didn't feel like I was in danger. With one swipe, I landed the cure on my first try.

Just moments later, Mustache Zombie stopped writhing and groaning. His eyes turned from gray to green. Unfortunately, his bushy mustache remained intact.

I cleared my throat. "Hi, Mustache, um, I mean . . . what's your name?"

"Matt." He blinked slowly. "What happened?"

I knelt down beside him. "What do you remember?"

"I was feeling sick. A whole bunch of us were. Pam had been throwing up for a while but felt too sick to even go home. And then she . . . she changed into something. There was screaming and fighting." His voice drifted off.

"Do you remember how you came to be hand-cuffed to this desk?"

"Not really, no." His eyes closed and he began to breathe deeply and slowly, like he was asleep.

"Sir." I gently pushed on his chest to wake him up. "Matt!"

His eyes opened again, but only halfway. "I've never been this tired in all my life."

"Yeah, you're probably going to take a long nap soon. I just need you to stay with me for a few more minutes."

He nodded once and his eyes half-closed.

"Do you have keys to get yourself out of these cuffs when you're not so tired anymore?"

"In my pocket," he croaked.

"Okay, one last question and then you can sleep. Detective Palamidis was supposed to meet a Veratrum employee today. Do you know anything about that?"

He moved his head a bit from side to side. "No."

"Do you know where I can find Detective Palamidis?"

"Started all of this," he mumbled.

"What?"

"Pam. Detective Palamidis is Pam."

The detective who might have some answers was the first police officer to turn into a zombie.

The dispatcher Willa cured was no help, either. She fell into a deep sleep almost immediately. Then Charlie texted that his house was still empty, and Marcus had a safe place to sleep for a while, so we decided to head there.

"Well, that was a dead end," Willa said, holding the police station door open for me. "Get it? *Dead* end? Because zombies are—"

"I get it." I eyeballed her. "Are you taking Charlie's place with dumb jokes?"

"Someone has to lighten things up." She stepped over a random, lost shoe. "Why are you so pessimistic about all this? You weren't like this last time."

"Um, because my town is filled with zombies?"

"But it had been filled with monsters and aliens, too, and we fixed that."

"Let's just head to Charlie's." I hated this feeling I was carrying inside me. That anything that could go wrong would. But I couldn't snap my fingers and make the feeling go away.

Willa started walking down Main Street, but I stopped her.

"We should cut through the common. It's a wide open space. We'll be able to see any threats easier." I thought about all the zombies stuck in Bodhi's Diner and knew lots of those little stores were probably keeping some zombies trapped. I didn't want to be surprised by an open door and a zombie horde.

"Sure," Willa said, hopping off the sidewalk onto the street. "We could even walk in the middle of the road. I haven't seen one car pass!"

The late afternoon sun moved lower in the sky as we strode toward the common. A golden retriever ran by us, not even stopping to get pet. Understandably.

A scream echoed from some distance away. I hated seeing the town I loved turned into this apocalyptic wasteland. Actually, it had only been a day, so the flowers were still pretty and the pumpkins on the stoops were fresh. But still.

"The coast looks clear," Willa said as we reached the common.

I pointed at the playground. "That swing is moving. Like someone walking by just bumped it."

"Probably the wind."

I chewed on my lower lip, unsure. "Okay, let's cut through."

My eyes moved left and right, and every now and then I looked over my shoulder. I didn't want to be taken by surprise. I had the game open on my phone so I could toss a cure quickly, but my battery was low. I hadn't known when I left the house this morning that I'd be using up my battery power to cure zombies around town.

Willa cut a straight path through the middle of the common.

"Let's bear right," I said. I wanted to keep space between us and the gazebo. A zombie could be hiding in there. We were better off heading a little bit right, toward the statue of John Wolcott, our town's founder.

As we passed the gazebo, I squinted at the shadows inside. Nothing.

"See?" Willa said. "It's fine. Things aren't as bad as they seem. Most of the zombies are stuck inside because they can't open doors."

Maybe she was right and my bad feeling was wrong. Maybe we'd make it home with no problem. Maybe—

"*Guuuuuuuuuhhhh.*"

I froze in place.

A shadow crept across the grass as a large someone—or something—came out from behind the statue. It was zombie Jason! Charlie's brother was two years older than we were and twice our size. His blond buzz cut and Wolcott Football sweatshirt looked the same, but that gray-eyed gaze and drooling mouth were dead giveaways.

"Launch!" I yelled.

"I'm opening the game!" Willa cried. "It'll just be a minute."

I lifted up my phone, game open, ready to attack the zombie with a cure. And the screen went black. The battery!

I gasped in horror. "My phone is dead." And soon I would be, too. Or . . . undead.

Zombie Jason lurched toward me, eyes alight with ravenous hunger. I remembered a ballet move Willa had used before to trip an evil alien. I stretched my leg out and connected with Jason's shin. He lost his balance, toppling to the ground. But his arm reached out, grabbing my ankle, and he brought me down with him.

Willa always was much better than I was at dance moves.

Caught in his tight grip, I squirmed and screamed. "Hurry, Willa!"

"I'm coming!" she said and aimed.

The red light arced out of her phone and landed on Jason's leg. He looked down at the spot and growled, mildly irritated, but not enough to let go of my leg. His eyes flared with hunger as he pulled me closer. His jaws snapped like an angry dog.

"Aim for the head!" I yelled. "Come on, Willa."

"I'm trying. I'm new at this!"

The only bad thing about our pact to not play *Zombie Town* was that now that we needed it, we all had a learning curve—one that could end with me becoming a Jason Tepper appetizer.

Willa launched another cure that landed somewhere in the grass beside us. It didn't help that I was writhing and squirming and Jason was moving to try to sink his teeth into me. But I wasn't going to lie still!

Another red light went sailing over our heads. Jason was so close now, his teeth only inches from my ankle.

And *BAM!* Direct hit.

Jason's grip on me relaxed, and I scrambled back up to standing. My breath came in ragged bursts.

"Sorry that took so long," Willa said.

"It's okay. You got him just in time."

My ankle throbbed where he'd been squeezing it. But it could have been a lot worse.

Jason slowly sat up, rubbing his eyes like a child awakening from a nap. "Bex? Where's my brother?"

I gripped his arm, which was the size of my leg, and helped him to his feet. "Charlie is at your house, where you need to be ASAP."

He swayed a bit. "I'm really tired."

Willa grabbed his other arm. "I know you're tired. And it's only going to get worse. But you need to stay awake until you get home because we can't carry you."

"Carry me," he said, confused. "Why would you carry—"

"Whoa there!" I said as he staggered. I put both hands on his shoulders to keep him from falling facedown. "We'll tell you all about it on the way."

Willa gave me a look. "We have to make it fast."

10

We slogged up the Teppers' driveway, Jason clinging to consciousness between us.

"Charlie, get your butt out here!" Willa shrieked.

The front door opened and a surprised Charlie dashed out to help us. "Jason! You're okay?"

"Yeah," Jason slurred. "Bex and Willa cured me, or whatever. But I need my bed. I need my bed right now."

It took the three of us to get him upstairs to his room. At the sight of his big, comfy bed, Jason sighed, said, "Finally," and fell face first into a pillow.

Charlie took his sneakers off, and the resulting smell drove us back downstairs pretty quickly. We collapsed into chairs around the dining room table. Charlie poured us glasses of water, which Willa and I chugged heartily. Getting Jason home had been quite the workout.

I wiped my mouth with the back of my hand. "How's Marcus?"

"Still sleeping in my room," Charlie said.

That worried me. What if the cure was some kind of Sleeping Beauty disease? What if Marcus slept forever?

"What should we do now?" Charlie asked, directing his question at me like I had a clue.

Willa clutched her stomach. "We should eat dinner."

At the mention of it, my stomach growled in response. I would give anything for one of my dad's big meals right now. My heart sank as I thought about his silly aprons and my mom losing her glasses when they were on the top of her head. How could you miss people so much when you just saw them yesterday?

"I can make spaghetti," Charlie said. He stood and started opening cabinets. "Yep, I have everything I need."

I forced a smile. "That would be great. Thanks."

Willa beamed. "Thanks, Charlie. You're the best."

While Charlie boiled water to cook the pasta, I charged my phone, and Willa called her house. I could hear her mother's frantic voice through the speaker, but Willa did a good job calming her down.

It hurt to think about my parents as zombies, wandering about town somewhere, their brains clicked off. I had to save them. I had to figure out a way.

"Just don't let Dad back in unless his eyes are brown again," Willa said to her mother. "Keep all the doors locked and you'll be fine."

After a muffled question, Willa answered, "Yeah, I'll sleep at Bex's. I'll call again tomorrow."

She ended the call and groaned.

"How are they?" I asked.

"My mom and my little brothers are fine but my dad turned. She pushed him outside with a broom. I told her to stay in and keep the doors locked."

I nodded. "They'll be safe."

"She doesn't want me crossing town to get back home so I'm going to stay at your house. Cool?"

"Of course," I said.

Charlie put down the spoon he'd been stirring the sauce with. "You guys are free to stay here. We'd be safer all together."

Willa grimaced. "If I stayed overnight at a boy's house with no parents, a zombie attack would pale in comparison to what I'd face at home."

"Point taken," Charlie said and poured the spaghetti into a strainer.

The meal Charlie spread out was pretty good—spaghetti and sauce, bread and butter, and cookies for dessert. I leaned back in the chair after I finished and patted my happy belly.

"Thanks," I said. "I needed this."

"I can make us all some French toast in the morning, too," Charlie offered.

"That would be great," Willa said, but her voice trailed off as she stared at something out the window.

I looked over my shoulder. My neighbor, Mrs. Sweeney, staggered down the street in what was now an easily recognizable zombie fashion.

"Poor Mrs. Sweeney." I moved to get up.

Charlie put a hand on my arm. "It's almost dark. It's not safe to run around curing people. Let's wait."

He was right. But it still felt awful to watch her wandering aimlessly. I wondered what her dog, William Shakespaw, had thought when his beloved owner turned into a zombie.

Willa chewed on her thumbnail. "At least they aren't like movie zombies. You know, limbs falling off, skin decaying."

"That will come with time," Charlie said.

I leaned forward. "What?"

"They've only been zombies for a day or so. What do you think will happen if we don't cure them soon?"

Gross. But he was right. Nature would take its toll eventually. All I could think about were my parents—slowly decaying faces, eyes dropping out, arms falling off. I pressed my fingers into my temples and forced myself to stop picturing these horrible images.

Willa stood and started piling up dishes. "We should head to your house before it gets too dark."

I agreed and scrubbed dishes, wishing I could scrub my mind. After we finished helping Charlie, we headed outside.

Willa took a long look at the decorations strewn across my front yard. "It looks like Halloween threw up on your grass."

I couldn't argue with that. I unlocked the front door and poked my head in. "Hello?"

"Who are you talking to?" Willa whispered. "Your zombie parents aren't here, right?"

No, they weren't. And the doors had all been closed so no new zombies could get in. Still, it felt like we weren't alone. We crept into the living room, closing the front door behind us. I couldn't put my finger on it, but something was off. There was a chill in the air, and I felt a tickle down my back.

And then my blood froze in my veins.

I'd left the living room window open when I dashed out this morning. That had let cool autumn air in, and sometime since then someone or something had pushed in the screen. When a noise came from the kitchen, it confirmed my worst fear.

We were *definitely* not alone.

11

"D o you hear that?" Willa whisper-screamed.

"It's coming from the kitchen," I said back, keeping my voice as hushed as possible. It had been a strange, scarfing noise. Like someone eating messily.

Definitely not a human sound.

I crept toward the doorway to the kitchen.

Willa grabbed my arm. "What are you doing?"

"I want to check it out." I slipped my phone out of the back pocket of my jeans and opened the *Zombie*

Town game. Maybe one of my parents had returned and crawled in through the window.

But then what were they eating so sloppily in the kitchen?

My imagination went to terrible places and I forced it back to the situation at hand. The game was loaded and ready. I held the phone up in front of me and charged through the doorway.

But the kitchen was empty. No one stood by the sink. No one by the island. No one sitting at the table.

The noise came again. A slurping, disgusting sound. Like a starving person had found their favorite meal but had no utensils.

It had to be coming from the other side of the island. That was the only part of the kitchen hidden from view. And whoever it was had to be eating . . . on the floor.

I wiped a drop of sweat that had formed on my forehead and tiptoed toward the island. Phone raised high, ready for zombie battle, I took a deep breath and rounded the corner.

William Shakespaw stood on the floor—all twenty pounds of white fur and wiggly butt. And he was eating our trash.

"It's only my neighbor's dog!" I called to Willa, who was still hiding around the side of the doorway.

"Is it a zombie dog?" she asked.

William looked up at me with his perpetually excited eyes, tail wagging, the remains of my parents' uneaten dinner hanging from his furry chin.

"No, he's just a regular dog. But he might be a little smelly. He's been going through the garbage."

Willa exhaled a relieved breath and came over to join us. "I can deal with smelly. Remember, I have two younger brothers."

I cleaned up the trash that William had spread all over the floor while Willa scratched behind his floppy ears.

"You must have been very scared when your owner turned into a big, bad, zombie, huh?" Willa asked in a baby voice. "But you climbed into Bex's house like a smart boy. Oh, yes, you're a good boy. Yes, you are."

William rolled onto his back so she could scratch his belly next.

The kitchen cleaned, I set about to double-check every door and window in the house. They were all closed and locked, except for the one William had used as an entry point, but I locked that one, too.

"We'll be totally safe tonight," I said.

Willa had cleaned the dog's dirty face and was now cuddling him in her arms. "He's sleeping upstairs with us."

"Sure." It wasn't a bad idea. Dogs had better hearing than humans, and he could alert us to any trouble.

Upstairs in my room, William made himself comfortable in a pile of my dirty laundry. Why sleep in a big comfortable bed when you could snuggle up to dirty socks? Oh, dogs never change.

Willa flopped onto the bed. "We haven't had a sleepover in years."

That was mainly because Willa had dumped me when she got popular, bullied me for a year or two, then more recently realized her mistake and earned my forgiveness. But whatever.

"Yeah, it's been a while," I said.

"Remember what we used to do at sleepovers?"

I thought for a moment. "You'd do my makeup and then we'd watch a horror movie." I cringed. "Kind of unnecessary right now. We're *in* a horror movie."

Willa smiled slowly. "Yeah, but without makeup."

I paused. "You can't be serious."

She gave me a hard stare.

Oh. She was serious. "Willa, no. I'm tired, and I want to go to sleep."

She knelt and clasped her hands. "But I'm anxious, and it will give me something productive to do with my nervous energy."

"I don't even have any makeup."

"Your mom has a ton. I saw it in the bathroom."

I knew this disagreement would end with Willa getting her way, so I figured I'd give in now so the whole debacle could be over sooner. "Okay, fine."

She clapped excitedly. "Yay!"

I sat still in my desk chair while Willa attacked my face with brushes and wands. Her expression was as serious as if she were painting the ceiling of the Sistine Chapel.

"Look up," she ordered.

I complied, mostly because I didn't want to get stabbed in the eye with an eyeliner pencil.

"You should totally let me do your makeup before the Halloween Dance," Willa said.

"Um, the town is overrun with zombies. I don't think we're having a dance."

She shrugged. "There's still time."

I didn't know how she could be so confident. And

even if we did have the dance, Marcus hadn't asked me. I was still kind of bummed out about that. I let out a small sigh.

"Stop frowning, you're scrunching your face."

"Sorry," I muttered.

Willa pointed a blush brush at me. "I don't understand why you're moping around waiting for Marcus to ask you to the dance."

"Because I like him. You know that!"

She rolled her eyes. "That's not what I mean. Why don't *you* ask *him*?"

I paused. "You would ask a boy out?"

"Of course! Why not?"

The idea had occurred to me. But every time I thought about it, this horrible feeling shot through my entire body. It was the same feeling I'd gotten when I'd waited in line for an hour to ride the Death Screamer roller coaster. Then when it was finally my turn, I freaked out and left. *That* feeling.

"You're scared," Willa said.

"Terrified," I admitted.

She put down the giant blush brush and picked up a smaller one. "You know he likes you."

"If he did, then why wouldn't he have asked me

by now? What was he waiting for?" I chewed on my lower lip. "He might have changed his mind. Maybe he doesn't like me anymore."

"Or maybe he's nervous. Just like you."

I thought about it. That might be true. But I pushed the thought away. "It doesn't matter anyway. I highly doubt we'll be having any dance any time soon. The priority now is survival. And we're not even sure that Marcus is going to be okay. He might not even wake up."

Willa threw her hands up in frustration, causing a cascade of powder to puff into the air from the brush she held. "You're catastrophizing."

I gave her a look. "Is that even a real word?"

"You're assuming the worst."

I crossed my arms. "Our town is full of zombies. If that's not a catastrophe—"

"Okay, okay, it's just . . . maybe don't assume the worst-case scenario. Have hope."

I didn't know how she was managing to stay so optimistic in the face of utter disaster.

She put all the makeup tools back in the bag and clapped her hands together. "Okay, done! Turn around and look in the mirror."

Speaking of the face of utter disaster . . .

I was expecting to look like a clown. Or a little kid trying too hard to look like an adult. But—shock of all shocks—I looked kind of . . . good.

Willa beamed. "What do you think?"

I didn't look like me. My freckles were gone and my face looked all smooth. My eyes seemed bigger and brighter. I looked like Bex's older, prettier sister.

"Be honest," Willa said.

"It's kind of nice but also kind of freaky."

Willa laughed. "Your eyebrows are goals, and they're totally natural!"

"Thanks? I think."

I preferred my regular face to the stranger in the mirror, but Willa seemed happy and relaxed, so I was glad I let her torture me. Now we could both go to sleep.

I headed toward bed and pulled the covers back.

"Um, what are you doing?" Willa asked.

I pointed at the bed as if it were obvious. "Going to sleep."

Willa gasped. "But you have to wash your face!"

"You *just* put the makeup on. Isn't that a waste?"

"Yeah, but if you sleep with it, you could get a pimple."

I slid into bed and pulled the covers up to my chin. "I could get bitten by a zombie tomorrow. A few zits don't scare me."

And with that small act of rebellion, I went to sleep. I only hoped that when I woke up the next day, Marcus would wake up, too.

woke early, light from the rising sun barely peeking through my window shade. William Shakespaw's light snoring from my laundry pile was strangely soothing. I didn't want to get up yet and wake Willa. But then I heard a noise in the house. William Shakespaw stirred and let out a low growl.

Willa shot up in bed. "What? Where? Who?"

"It's okay," I said, pushing myself up on my elbows.

"No, it's not," she insisted, her hair plastered to the side of her face. "I heard something."

I heard it, too. But I recognized it right away. I'd been listening to that sound my whole life. It was the loud, sometimes clumsy, footfall of Charlie clomping up my stairs. I always knew when it was Charlie and not one of my parents or other friends.

"It's only Charlie," I said. "He must have awakened and—"

Willa shot out of bed. "It could be a zombie."

"The doors and windows were locked. No zombie could get in."

"Then how could Charlie come in?"

"He probably used our hidden key. He's done it before."

William Shakespaw growled, baring his tiny white teeth.

"Grab a weapon," Willa said. "Any weapon."

"I'm telling you we don't need a weapon." I rubbed my face with my hands and then choked back a laugh when I saw what she'd chosen. "Is that a mascara wand? What are you going to do, lengthen his lashes?"

"It's the first thing I found!" she cried.

William stood up, his little doggie head cocked to the side.

The intruder delivered two swift knocks on the door, then swung it open.

Willa screamed and pointed her mascara wand.

Charlie gave her a strange look. "What are you doing?"

Willa dropped the cosmetic weapon to her side. "Just . . . getting ready."

"Good," Charlie said. "We were hoping you two were awake."

My heart rose up into my throat. "We?"

Another set of footsteps clomped up the stairs, and Marcus poked his head into the room from behind Charlie. "Hi!"

"You're okay?" I cried.

"I was undead, then I slept like the dead, and now I'm totally back to normal. All cured, thanks to you."

Relief rushed through me, and I couldn't help myself. I ran to Marcus and threw my arms around his neck. "I'm so glad!"

Then, realizing I'd been hugging him for a weirdly long amount of time, I pulled back and grinned. "Sorry."

He smiled back. "It's all good." Then he looked at me strangely, like he was trying to figure something out.

Oh. I still had that makeup on!

"Willa did it," I said quickly. "She put makeup on me."

"Ah!" he said, nodding. "You look pretty, don't get me wrong. But I miss your freckles. Is that weird?"

I laughed. "Not weird, no. You like my freckles?"

He shrugged. "Yeah, they're *you*."

I felt a blush spread across my face—and not the makeup kind. Willa gave me a knowing look.

"So," Charlie said, breaking the awkward silence. "I brought the ingredients for French toast. Who wants breakfast?"

Downstairs, Jason was already picking his way through my cabinets as we walked into the kitchen.

"Glad to see you're better, too!" I said.

Jason turned around, mouth full of cookies, and said, "Mamphs. Grad yoo cuu meh."

Willa raised her eyebrows. "Are you sure he's cured?"

"Yeah," Charlie said. "He's just rude."

Jason wiped the cookie crumbs off his mouth

and tried again after he finished chewing. "I said, 'Thanks. Glad you cured me.'"

"And we basically carried you all the way home," Willa added.

"I owe you one," he said, turning back to the cabinet for more food.

"Is ravenous hunger a side effect of the cure?" I asked.

"No, that's just normal Jason," Charlie said.

Charlie whipped up an amazing breakfast, and we all sat around my dining room table, like a family, to eat it. I still missed my parents terribly, but having my best friends here together helped a lot. And knowing the cure worked filled me with hope for the first time since this disaster began.

I took a sip from my orange juice. "Okay, let's plan."

Charlie cleared his throat. "The good news is that we can cure the zombies. The undead turn into the merely unawake. And then they're completely back to normal after a lot of sleep."

"But the bad news," Willa said, "is that there are too many of them, and they have to be cured one at a time."

"And every time we go out there to cure someone, we put ourselves at risk," Marcus said.

Jason stabbed a piece of French toast with his fork. "What if we all get bitten, and there's no one left to throw the cures?"

My throat tightened. "Then the whole town is doomed."

Charlie stared down at his plate, frowning as he chewed. I knew that look. His brain was working hard.

I bumped his elbow with mine. "What are you thinking about?"

"Science class."

Jason rolled his eyes. "Really? Right now? Such a nerd."

Charlie scratched his chin. "We learned about viruses the other day. They require a host to survive and multiply."

"Just like this zombie video game virus," I said. "It needs a host to survive, and it uses that host to replicate—by biting other potential hosts."

"So we need to replicate the cure," Marcus said, following along.

Charlie nodded. "With regular viruses, our bodies

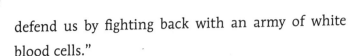

defend us by fighting back with an army of white blood cells."

Willa dabbed at her mouth with a napkin. "So we make more white blood cells—us—to cure the zombies."

I sat up straight in my seat. "Right! We can't cure the whole town ourselves. But if we can find people we know are good gamers and cure them, we could build up a team." I looked around at all my friends and smiled for the first time in what felt like days. "We'll create an army of gamers."

13

Now that we knew the cure really worked and we had our gamer army plan, I felt more ready to set out into the day. We all dressed and met outside on Charlie's front lawn.

"We should split up," Charlie said, "cover more ground, cure more zombies faster."

"Any ideas who to target?" Willa asked.

"Mrs. Dorsey probably went to work and turned there," I said. Mrs. Dorsey was my favorite librarian and a hardcore gamer. She'd helped us in the past with other mobile game disasters, so I knew she'd be on board.

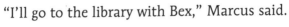

"I'll go to the library with Bex," Marcus said.

I tried not to blush. And failed.

"I could go to my friend Chloe's house and cure her," Willa offered.

"I'll go with you," Charlie said. "Then we'll hit a couple of other friends' houses. I think some people who played the game live near Chloe."

"I know a bunch of kids on the football team who played," Jason said. "I can go alone. I mean, look at me." He flexed his biceps.

I stifled a laugh, and Charlie just shook his head.

"Okay, Gamer Squad," Marcus said. "Time to build our army. Find them, cure them, enlist them. We'll fix this town, one zombie at a time."

I plastered a smile on my face and exchanged enthusiastic high fives with the team. But on the inside I knew it wouldn't be that easy.

It felt strange to walk downtown alone with Marcus. I walked alone with Charlie all the time, but this was different. I didn't have to think when I was with Charlie. But with Marcus, I was nervous. I didn't want to say anything dumb.

Here we were, walking through a desolate town searching for zombies, and my hands were sweating because I was scared to look silly in front of my crush. I really had to examine my priorities.

"Um, so," I said, searching my brain for anything to bring an end to the silence. "Any word on your parents?" Marcus was an only child like me, another thing we had in common. And his parents had also come down with the sickness that first night.

"When I left for school, they were still in their bedroom with the door closed. They'd been sick all night. So they're probably locked in the house, which is fine. They're safer that way until I can get back and cure them."

Safer than mine, I thought, who were out who knows where.

The sadness must have shown on my face because Marcus winced and said, "Sorry."

I shrugged. "It's okay. I'll find my parents and save them."

"And I'll help," he said.

As we neared the common, a zombie woman wearing a long pink housecoat staggered toward us.

"I've got this," I said, whipping my phone out of my pocket and launching a cure. I had the game loaded and ready.

My first shot was a direct hit. The woman stumbled back a few steps, then shook her head as human consciousness returned. Well, barely. She was almost asleep on her feet.

"What am I doing in the middle of the road?" she asked, confusion settling over her features.

I coughed into my hand. "You were heading to the store to get some cold medicine."

"Was I? Yes, that must have been it. I do feel sick." She frowned.

"A terrible flu is going through town," I said. "You should probably head home and sleep it off."

"Yes, you're right," she said dreamily. Then she teetered off.

"Well done," Marcus said, as we started walking again. "You've really got this zombie curing thing down."

"I'm definitely not as nervous as I was with my first one." I gave him a look and he laughed.

"Was I a scary zombie?" he asked. "I wish I could have seen myself."

"Yeah, you were pretty terrifying. You were all like . . ." I opened my jaw wide and made groaning and growling noises.

Marcus laughed so hard he had to cover his mouth. "You're right, that *is* horrifying."

"Hey, if it weren't for me, you'd still be like that."

"I still can't believe it." He shook his head in amazement. "You went into that hallway without even knowing if the cure would work. I could have bitten you. You are so astonishingly brave."

There I went again, blushing so hard I was probably as red as a lobster. I could feel it in my cheeks.

Marcus put a hand on my shoulder. "Hey, maybe later today we could head to the school to cure whoever is there. And you can see that game I made that I wanted to show you before our town became zombie town."

I chuckled. "Yeah, sure." That game was really important to him. Even while all of this was happening.

We were almost to the library doors when a groan came from behind the large oak tree on the front lawn.

"One up ahead," I said, grabbing for my phone.

"Can I do this one?" Marcus asked. "I downloaded

the game back at the house, but I need to get some experience."

"Sure." I motioned with my hand for him to move in front of me.

A boy came lumbering down the grass toward the sidewalk, wheezing like he was ninety and not nine. He wore pajamas with planets on them and no shoes.

"Poor kid," Marcus said.

"You know what to do, right?" I asked.

"Yeah. Aim for the head."

Marcus held up his phone and swiped. The first couple tries went completely off, but he got the hang of it after that. The red light arced in the air, hitting the boy in the arm. He momentarily staggered but kept coming toward us, a line of drool slipping from his open mouth.

I gripped my phone tighter, ready to provide backup if necessary. But Marcus got a direct hit with his next throw.

The little boy blinked slowly and rubbed his eyes. "Why am I outside the library in my pajamas?"

I figured I'd go with the truth. An adult might not believe me, but a kid would. Kids' minds are still open.

"You played a lot of *Zombie Town*, right?" I asked.

He looked at me suspiciously. "Yeah."

"Everyone who played the game turned into a zombie. But we can cure them by using the game."

He narrowed his eyes. "Playing the game cures real zombies?"

"Yeah," Marcus said. "Hey, buddy, you're going to start to feel real tired soon."

The boy nodded his head sluggishly. "I do."

"Do you live close?" Marcus asked.

He pointed toward a nearby side street. "Right there."

Good. He'd make it, no problem. "Go home," I ordered. "If your parents are zombies, use the game. Toss cures at them just like you do with fake zombies. Aim for their heads. Then take a long nap. Everything will be fine."

The boy's lower lip curled down in fear. "How do you know everything will be okay?"

Marcus placed a hand on the boy's shoulder and smiled. "Because the Gamer Squad is on the case."

Reassured, the little boy smiled sleepily and nodded. Then he headed off toward his house.

"Think they'll all be that easy?" Marcus asked.

I look up at the brick arch above the entrance to the library. "Not a chance."

14

The front door to the library was unlocked, so we pushed it open and tiptoed inside.

"You think Mrs. Dorsey is here?" Marcus whispered.

I nodded. "She played the game, so she must have the sickness. She tends to come in early, even before opening hours, because different groups meet in the event room."

I pointed to the bulletin board on the wall, which showed all the groups that held their meetings in the event room downstairs—from sewing circles to book clubs, Scrabble tournaments to the Teen Advisory Board. From the looks of the note on the wall, the Teen Advisory Board was supposed to meet yesterday before school to vote on next month's movie night selection.

Marcus said, "She probably came in even though she wasn't feeling well, to unlock to the doors. And then . . ." his voice trailed off.

My favorite librarian was somewhere in this building, and she was a zombie.

The library was quiet—even more so than usual—which was good. We didn't need to deal with zombie Mrs. Dorsey *and* a whole bunch of zombie patrons.

We moved past the eerily empty checkout desk. The bank of computer terminals sometimes had a waiting line but now they were all empty, their screensavers swirling.

A shuffling sound from the stacks caught my attention. Marcus and I looked at each other.

"The Mystery aisle?" he suggested.

"I think it's closer." I pointed. "Sci-Fi."

We edged toward that aisle, peeking around stacks of books. The grunting noises got louder as we neared Sci-Fi. We stopped right before the aisle's opening. My heart sped up. I pulled out my phone. My finger trembled as I held it above the screen, waiting to swipe.

Marcus readied his phone as well. He looked at me and I mouthed, "Now!"

We jumped into the row, startling Mrs. Dorsey, who was indeed a zombie. Her head was flopped to the side, and that face I'd always found so warm and welcoming was now slack and terrifying. Her gray eyes flared as she lurched toward us.

Marcus and I stood shoulder to shoulder—well, not quite because he was so tall—but we took up the whole row. We swiped, quickly and efficiently, tossing cures at Mrs. Dorsey as she got closer and angrier. One arc of red light hit her arm and she lashed out, knocking a pile of books from the shelf to the ground. A zombie horror novel fell on my feet.

Fitting.

We launched again and again until finally one of our shots was a direct hit.

Mrs. Dorsey stopped moving, a stunned expression on her face. She gazed at us, recognition dawning. "Bex? What just happened? I feel like I have a hole in my memory."

"You were a zombie," Marcus said, matter-of-factly.

She swayed on her feet, from shock, the illness, or a combination of both. I knew that the extreme fatigue was hitting her hard, and we only had a few minutes before she'd be asleep.

"The new game, *Zombie Town*, turned all the players into actual zombies," I explained. "And when they bite others, they turn as well."

She gasped, her hand fluttering to her mouth.

I continued, "You're going to get very tired and sleep, possibly for a long time. But when you wake up, you have to help us fight. The game caused this, but the game can fix it. You toss the cures, same as always. Try to cure people you know who are good at the game, so they can help us, too. Aim for the head."

"We're building a gamer army," Marcus said.

Mrs. Dorsey nodded quickly. "My whole book club played. I'll cure them as soon as I can." Her eyes rolled back and then refocused. "But first . . . I need a nap."

We helped her to the floor. I found a sweatshirt in the lost and found and put that under her head as a pillow.

"She'll be safe here," I said. "But I'd like her to have her phone nearby when she wakes up."

"Is it downstairs in her office? In a purse or something?" Marcus asked.

I nodded. "Most likely. Let's go look."

We trotted downstairs and checked the office. Sure enough, a big, black leather handbag sat on the floor behind a desk. I opened the zipper and pulled out her phone. "Got it."

We left the office and closed the door behind us. "After we bring this upstairs, where do you want to go next?" I asked.

A loud bang came from the door to the event room. Almost like it was in response to my voice.

Marcus reached out and tried to turn the knob. "It's not locked."

"That means a human could open it."

The bang came again, louder, like someone slammed themselves against the door.

"Sounds like your typical confused zombie," Marcus said. "Should we cure it?"

I shrugged. "Why not? We're on a roll."

I readied my phone and nodded to Marcus, who

was gripping the door knob. He turned it and pulled opened the door. But we were wrong.

Someone wasn't at the door. It was a zombie horde.

I recognized my friend Isaac and a few other kids from school. Some had been players, some had been bitten. But two things were clear: yesterday morning's Teen Advisory Board meeting had been an actual nightmare, and Marcus and I were in over our heads.

Marcus tried to shut the door, but the zombies rushed at the opening, pushing him. I moved backward until the heel of my shoe hit the wall. Isaac lunged at Marcus, and he reeled back, falling to the floor. I swiped as fast as I could, trying to cure the zombies in front of me so I could get to him. I couldn't watch Marcus be bitten again!

Four zombies leaned over him, teeth chomping.

Marcus rolled between their feet. Confused, two bent-over zombies bonked heads. While they growled at each other, Marcus ran back into the event room and quickly climbed on top of a table.

"Join me!" he shouted.

Marcus threw some cures as cover while I ran to

him. The zombies tried their best to dodge and fight the arcs of red light. I scrambled up the table and faced the dwindling horde. Two girls and one boy had already been cured and were swaying on their feet, confused by the scene in front of them.

Three more zombies heaved toward us, arms raised in front of them. Even though the table gave us some height, they'd still be able to reach our legs. Marcus and I swiped repeatedly, but the zombies were staggering left and right. It would be helpful for aiming purposes if they didn't walk like, well, zombies.

My heart pumped wildly in my chest the closer they got. I went to swipe up again and the phone slipped out of my sweaty hand.

"No!" I screamed, while I watched it fall to the floor below as if it were happening in slow motion.

Marcus stayed focused, taking out two more zombies. Only one remained—my friend Isaac. He reached the edge of the table and clasped his hand hard around my ankle. He pulled and I pulled back— it was like the worst game of tug of war I'd ever played. Up on the table, I had nothing to hold on to. I was going to lose my balance.

Just in time, Marcus lodged a direct hit, and Isaac froze in place.

He looked down at his hand, still gripping my ankle, then pulled it back. "What? Why?"

The other kids behind him were also in various states of shock, rubbing their foreheads and muttering to themselves.

"Time to recruit our army," I said to Marcus. "You want to give the speech?"

15

Marcus gave a rousing speech to the library's Teen Advisory Board. They agreed to our plan and seemed ready to help us save the town—after a giant group nap, that is. I picked up my phone—unbroken from the fall, thank goodness—then slipped Mrs. Dorsey's phone into her hand as she slept. And then we headed back out.

As we walked downtown, I limped for the first few steps. My ankle was kind of sore.

Marcus blew out a breath. "That was a bit too close for my liking."

"Agreed. Maybe splitting up wasn't the best idea." We could take down a zombie when it was two to one, but who knew what hid behind every closed door.

"I wonder how Charlie and Willa are doing."

Just as Marcus said the words, they came around a corner. The neat bun Willa had started the morning with was half pulled out, and Charlie had twigs in his hair.

I reached up and pulled one of them out. "I think your morning went about as great as ours."

Charlie rubbed his face and groaned. "It would have been nice to know beforehand that Chloe's big sister was having a sleepover on zombie night. We were attacked by a group of undead ballerinas."

"The terrifying tutus," Willa said, wagging her eyebrows.

Charlie busted out laughing. "I will never forget that."

I looked back and forth between them. "What?"

"Well, one of them came out and . . . forget it. It's a long story," Charlie said. "What happened to you guys?"

"Teen Advisory Board ambush," Marcus explained.

But I was still stuck on the fact that Charlie and Willa were giggling over their story. It was strange for Charlie to have an inside joke with a girl who wasn't me. Then again, Marcus and I were building our own stories, and that didn't lessen my friendship with Charlie at all. This was just something I'd have to get used to.

And in the meantime, there were zombies to cure.

Charlie's phone trilled, and he took a peek. "Text from Jason. He cured a bunch of football players. He's moving on to lacrosse next. He knows guys who play the game."

"Where should we head next to recruit?" Willa asked.

What I wanted to do was find and cure my parents. But I had no idea where they could be. They weren't locked in like Marcus's. They weren't stuck at work—they hadn't gone to work. They could be anywhere.

A cry echoed across the empty street. I'd heard a few screams here and there this morning, which was to be expected in a zombie apocalypse. But this voice was close by and so desperate. It pulled at my heartstrings.

"Let's find that person," I said.

We all nodded and grunted in agreement.

It wasn't hard to follow the sound. The person—a girl, from what I could tell—was crying hysterically. We marched down the center of Main Street with a good view of all of downtown. But no one else stood in the street or sidewalks.

Then it came again. "Please, someone! Please help!" And the voice sounded slightly familiar.

I pointed. "She's in the alley between the flower shop and the diner."

We charged over, and I kept one hand on my phone. Zombies couldn't talk, but she might have been cornered by one. But when we peered around the side of the brick wall, we found a girl all alone. She sat with her knees pulled up, her face buried.

"Hey," I said gently. "We're here to help."

Then she lifted her face up. It was my friend, Vanya! And I knew exactly why she was crying.

Vanya darted over to me and threw her arms around my neck. "Oh, Bex. Oh, it's terrible. My parents . . . the whole restaurant . . ."

"I know," I said. "I saw."

She pulled back. "What's wrong with them?"

Vanya's thick black hair was stuck to the tears on her cheeks. I tucked it behind her ears. "That game, *Zombie Town*, turned people into zombies."

Her dark eyes widened. "But how? Why?"

"That's a long story and something we hope to get to the bottom of," Charlie said. "But the important thing is, we can save everybody."

Her lower lip trembled. "How?"

I explained that the game that had turned them could be used to cure them, and I shared our plan for building a gamer army.

"So we'll head into the restaurant and cure them as quickly as possible," I said. "And then you can watch over them while they sleep and make sure the gamers join our ranks once they're back up and healthy."

Vanya nodded quickly. "Okay. I can do that."

I looked at Charlie, Willa, and Marcus. "Ready, Gamer Squad?"

Even though there were four of us, we were outnumbered by the amount of zombies in the restaurant. We needed a strategy. Thankfully, Vanya could help us with that, too.

"There's a back door into the restaurant, right?" I asked.

"Yeah," Vanya said. "I have a key."

I rubbed my chin. "Okay. One of us should cause a disturbance at the front. They'll all come to the big window. They did that earlier when Willa and I walked by. And then the rest of us can ambush them from behind through the back door."

"I'll go to the front and distract them," Willa volunteered.

Marcus, Charlie, and I took Vanya's key to the back door and quietly unlocked it. We stood at the end of the alley, waiting for Willa to make a ruckus. Soon enough, I heard her pounding on the glass of the front window.

"Come bite me, you big dumb zombieheads!"

She was usually better with her insults, but I'd give her a pass since she was under pressure.

"Ready?" Charlie whispered.

I slowly turned the knob and poked my head inside. The back door led into the kitchen. I didn't see any zombies, but I heard them. They were all in the dining area, shuffling and groaning toward Willa's shouting.

"It's safe," I said, keeping my voice low.

We tiptoed inside the kitchen. One of the stove's

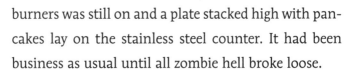

burners was still on and a plate stacked high with pancakes lay on the stainless steel counter. It had been business as usual until all zombie hell broke loose.

Marcus turned off the burner and led the way through the narrow kitchen toward the dining room. The two were separated by a wooden swinging door with a circular window. He took a look, then turned back to us. "They're all at the front, looking at Willa."

I could hear them and their varied groans and screeches. It sounded like an angry brawl of incoherent cats. And we were about to bust right in. I shook off my nerves and pushed past my growing dread. "Let's do this."

We did our best to sneak up behind them while they were focused on Willa, who, for some reason, had moved on from yelling at them and was instead practicing her dance moves. I shrugged. Whatever worked.

I whispered, "Three, two, one."

The three of us started launching cures as fast as our fingers let us. As soon as those red arcs of light hit a few of the zombies, they turned away from Willa (who was now singing a Beyoncé song) and headed toward us.

Uh-oh. It was about to get real.

A white-haired lady with some seriously bad posture, even for a zombie, grunted as she shuffled toward Marcus. He cured her relatively quickly, but there were a lot more to go.

Chaos quickly erupted. The restaurant was already small, but with a group of clumsy zombies barreling around, it seemed tiny. Chairs got knocked over. Plates of food went flying. Cups of coffee and orange juice fell to the floor, which made it slippery. Sliding zombies only added to the confusion as they careened into one another.

Willa came through the front door, phone blazing, to help us out. Vanya watched helplessly from the street while we battled. I should have had her download the game in case we needed her help. But I didn't think. She wasn't a gamer. Her parents were the ones in her family who had played.

Speaking of her parents, her father lumbered toward me in his white apron. I threw back-to-back cures, landing the second one. But while my attention was focused on curing Mr. Patel, a zombie customer with a crooked trucker hat grabbed me by the shoulders and leaned in.

I recoiled from his nasty zombie breath and yelled, "Little help, guys!"

Willa twirled around and launched three cures in a row, turning him before he could turn me.

Charlie was backed into a corner, trying his best to cure Vanya's mom while another zombie closed in. His hungry eyes flashed. He was looking at Charlie the way that I looked at pizza.

I leapt over a fallen zombie and landed a cure in midair.

"Wow!" Charlie said. "That was awesome!"

I beamed. "I know, right?" Now was not the time to be humble.

But just when I thought we had a handle on the situation, things turned bad. Some of the cured customers started to panic and scream. One of them managed to get bitten again in the chaos. They were running around, bouncing off chairs and skidding into one another. I couldn't tell who was cured and who wasn't, and they were blocking our throws at the zombies who were left.

I took a deep breath, then climbed on top of the long diner counter. This would be a good time to know how to whistle, but it was one of those things I just couldn't do. I'd taught myself two programming languages but when I tried to whistle, it sounded like someone repeatedly blowing out a trick candle on a cake.

I tried yelling instead. "Everyone who is not a zombie and not part of the Gamer Squad, get into the kitchen! It is safe there. Wait and we'll take care of the rest. Go! Go now!"

Thankfully, Mr. and Mrs. Patel listened, rushing into the kitchen, the door swinging behind them. The cured customers followed their lead. Only zombies were left in the dining area, slugging along slowly, following their prey toward the kitchen.

"Now's our chance!" I yelled.

With the undead separated from the living, it was easier for us to aim our cures. Marcus, Charlie, and Willa hopped up on the counter with me. We aimed and fired over and over. Long arcs of red light bounced around the room until finally every zombie was cured. Confused, but cured.

Vanya warily entered the room. "Is it over?"

I jumped down off the counter and wiped some sweat from my forehead. "Yeah, but everyone is pretty freaked out. Are you ready for your part?"

She nodded quickly. "Definitely. And my parents will help. I'll explain what's going on and after everyone has a rest, I'll make sure they head out to cure more people."

With that taken care of, I looked around for the rest of the Gamer Squad so we could move on to our next target. Marcus and Charlie were by my side but Willa wasn't there. She'd jumped off the counter. But where had she run off to?

The swinging door to the kitchen opened and Willa emerged, carrying the untouched plate of pancakes we'd seen on our way in. She picked one up with her hand and tore off a bite.

Charlie stifled a laugh, and I gave her a look that said *Really?*

"What?" she said through a full mouth. "Zombie-hunting makes me hungry. A girl's gotta eat."

16

We took a well-earned break to stuff our faces and charge our phones. Then we were back at it, roaming the streets of Wolcott, looking for zombies to cure.

This had turned into a weird world.

Walking down the middle of the road, four across, phones held out like weapons, I felt like we were starring in one of those old westerns. But with cell-phones. And zombies. The others chatted excitedly

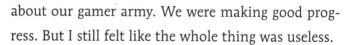

about our gamer army. We were making good progress. But I still felt like the whole thing was useless.

"Hey." Charlie nudged me with his elbow. "You're quiet. What's up?"

I thought about saying "nothing" but my best friend knew me too well. I took a deep breath. "Let's say we get through today without getting zombified. We create our gamer army and we save the town. It's a long shot, but for argument's sake, let's pretend that's all going to work."

"Okay . . ." Charlie said.

"Then what's to stop Veratrum from zombifying everyone again? Or releasing a new game that turns us into vampires? Or ghosts? It just seems never-ending."

I hated this pessimistic feeling that had overtaken me. I'd always been such a hopeful person. But I was also a realist, and it was hard to find hope right now. I only wished that Charlie wouldn't be disappointed in me for how I was feeling.

"I agree," he said.

I turned to look at him, my mouth agape. "What?"

"I've been worried about that, too. I'm not risking

my life and going through all of this just to have Veratrum throw it all away with their next game."

"If you're feeling the same way, then why aren't you sad?" *Like me*, I thought.

A crooked smile spread across his face. "Because I have a plan."

Intrigued, I asked, "Oh, yeah? What?"

"Hey, you guys!" Willa interrupted. "Check it out."

A dark blue car was parked halfway up the sidewalk, and shadows inside of it were moving.

We strolled toward it. Marcus jogged up and took a peek in the window.

"Four high school dudes," Marcus called over his shoulder. "All wearing Wolcott Baseball jackets."

"All zombies?" Charlie asked as we reached him.

"Yup," Marcus answered and stepped back so we could all take a look.

I recognized a kid named Julian who lived on my street. The four teens thrashed and squirmed in anger, clawing at the windows.

"Did they all change at once?" Willa asked with pity in her voice.

I shrugged. "Either that or one turned and bit the others. Who knows? I'm just glad they can't open doors."

"We should cure them," Charlie said. "They could join our army."

We all quickly agreed and readied ourselves for battle. Marcus reached out and opened the driver's side door.

Willa pinched her nose. I covered my mouth, gagging. It was the putrid smell of . . . THE UNSHOWERED. Granted, those movie zombies with rotting limbs probably smelled worse. But four teenage boys who'd been doing a lot of writhing in a warm car and not a lot of bathing were a close second.

Seeing that a way out had suddenly appeared—with a tasty meal on the other side—all four zombies attempted to fit through the open car door at once. And they got stuck.

Sighing, Marcus opened the back door.

One of the zombies pulled away and went for the other door, lessening the pressure and allowing all of them to climb for freedom. Or fall out onto the road, in one case.

"Spread out!" I yelled. "Everyone focus on your closest zombie."

There were four of them and four of us, odds I liked much better than our odds at the diner. My zombie was the one that had emerged from the back door. He lumbered toward me, one shoulder lower than the other. I fired a few cures, getting him easily.

The others seemed to be doing just as well. Willa's zombie was getting kind of close, so I aimed my phone to help.

"I got this!" she shouted, and with one last toss, her zombie baseball player stopped moving and did the slow blink of the newly conscious.

The four guys looked at us like *we* were the weird ones, even though we were all standing together in the middle of the street. Well, we were standing. They were swaying with fatigue.

One scratched the top of his head. "What happened to my car, man? It's up on the curb."

"I don't remember, dude," another said.

They gazed at us like we had all the answers. And we did, but I was getting tired of telling the same story.

"Have you ever seen *Zombieland*?" I asked. "*28 Days Later? Night of the Living Dead? World War Z?*"

The closest one shook his head. "I'm more of a comedy guy."

I sighed. I'd have to tell the same story.

"I'll explain this time," Willa said, sensing my frustration.

I took the opportunity to sidle up to Charlie. "So about that plan you mentioned."

"Let's keep building our army today," he said. "We'll go over the plan at dinner tonight. I hope you don't mind spaghetti again. It's really all I know how to make."

One of the players took his baseball jacket off, and I got a fresh whiff of uncontained body odor.

"As long as it smells better than that, I'll be happy."

"Hey," Marcus said, pointing at something behind me. "We've got another one."

I turned around and saw a woman with tight curly hair lumbering toward us. She was dragging one foot and growling—definitely zombified. But even more interesting, she was a police officer in uniform.

"I'll do it," Marcus offered.

"I'll be your backup," I said.

It was amazing how far we'd come. Taking on a zombie one-on-one had been terrifying the first day. But now it was as easy as ordering a pizza. Marcus held out his phone and tossed cures. The first one went wild, but the second landed on her right shoulder, and the third square in the face.

"Got her!" he called.

She swayed on her feet. Marcus and I ran to either side of her, to help her stay standing.

"She can take her nap in the car with the other guys," Marcus said.

"Good plan." I didn't want to leave her on the side of the road. But she was definitely departing the Land of the Conscious soon.

Her mouth opened and closed as she tried to make words. "What . . . happened?"

"It's a long story," I said. "Involving zombies and—" I broke off as I saw her name badge.

"What?" Marcus asked.

"You're Detective Palamidis?" I asked.

She nodded slowly.

"You had an appointment today with a whistle-blower from Veratrum, right?"

She gave me a strange look, probably wondering how I could have known that. "It didn't happen," she slurred. "Never got the chance."

Marcus and I were now mostly carrying her toward the car. She could barely stand on her own. I needed to get as much information as I could before she fell asleep.

"Do you know anything about what info they had? Anything that could help us?"

She narrowed her eyes, not trusting me.

"Veratrum did this," I said between gritted teeth. "I want to stop them. But I need to know what I'm dealing with."

She slumped into Marcus's arms, her eyes rolling up.

"Please!" I yelled. "Do you know anything?"

"The deal," she croaked. "Check out their big contract. There's something there."

And then she was gone, her breath coming deep and slow. Marcus hefted her into the car with the others. I wouldn't be able to get any more information.

"What was all that about?" Charlie asked.

I explained, "When Willa and I were at the police station, we saw that Detective Palamidis had an appointment today with a whistleblower from Veratrum. Someone wanted to talk."

"That was Palamidis?" Willa pointed at the now sleeping detective.

"Yeah, but I wasn't able to get much information. Just something about a contract."

Marcus had been conspicuously quiet. But now he spoke up. "That's okay. Now we have somewhere to start."

17

By the afternoon, we were experienced zombie hunters. We liked finding singles because four against one took care of the job pretty quickly. And we made sure not to open any doors that had more than four zombies inside. Tomorrow, when our army awoke, we'd be able to take on even more. And before long, the whole town would be cured.

That was the plan anyway.

After we cured the baseball players in the car,

we visited the houses of a few more gamer friends and cured them one by one. Then we saved a group of roving elderly ladies who'd apparently been in a salon, their hair still up in foil. Between the Gamer Squad and Jason, we cured dozens. But there was still a long way to go. And the larger Veratrum problem remained.

When we came home from our long day, I showered the filth and sweat off me. Willa took a turn, too, and then we headed next door to Charlie's house for dinner.

Charlie's kitchen was filled with the wonderful smell of Grandpa Tepper's extra-garlicky spaghetti sauce. Charlie had defrosted some they'd stored in the freezer, and my stomach growled as I sat at the table and waited. Every muscle in my body was sore and tired, so it felt good to sit and do nothing for a few minutes.

Marcus, however, had his laptop open on the table. His fingers tapped at the keyboard so fast, I thought it would burst into flames.

"What are you doing?" Willa asked. "I don't think teachers will be expecting our homework done."

"I'll tell you soon," he muttered, unwilling to

be distracted. A crease had formed in his forehead. Whatever he was doing, he was in deep.

"Dinner is served!" Charlie announced.

I piled my plate high and scarfed down the pasta like I hadn't eaten in days. Zombie-hunting and curing sure built up an appetite. We all ate greedily and messily, not pausing to speak, only grunt. Jason took down enough spaghetti for a family of four, but then again, that was sort of his normal everyday diet.

As our feast slowed to a stop, I leaned back in my chair. "So what were you working on, Marcus?"

He wiped his mouth with a napkin and cleared his throat. "I examined the source code of the game, hoping I could find a way to somehow reverse this."

Willa sat up straight. "And?" she said excitedly.

He shook his head. "No such luck. The code is weird, and I couldn't find anything we can reverse."

A heavy silence filled the room.

"However," Marcus said, "then I decided to do some research on Veratrum and their company history, based on what that detective mentioned."

I leaned forward, putting my elbows on the table. "Did you find anything suspicious?"

He pushed his plate aside and opened his laptop

on the table. "When they first opened for business, right here in Wolcott, they had four employees."

"Seems normal for a small start-up," Charlie said.

"Yeah," Marcus agreed. "They made a couple of cheesy little apps. Nothing that took off. Their work didn't reach any level of popularity, and they weren't making money."

"Then what happened?" Jason asked.

"They got a contract," Marcus said. "A big one. It gave them enough money to hire a hundred people and produce their first big, popular game."

"*Monsters Unleashed*," I said.

"Is that not normal?" Willa asked. "Getting a contract like that?"

"Usually a small company would get an investor," Charlie said.

"Yeah, or a venture capital firm," Marcus said. "That's what my dad does. But this is different."

"How so?" I asked.

"Because the money isn't from a regular investor. It's from a defense contracting company."

"Like a company that makes weapons and stuff?" Jason asked as he ripped off another bite of garlic bread. "Cool."

"Not cool." I sat back in my seat, my brain working on overdrive. "If the contract was from a company like that, they'd want something in return. But what would they want from a game developer?"

Charlie raked his fingers through his hair. "What if these aren't just games? What if the monsters, aliens, and zombies aren't accidents?"

"Great," Willa said. "Not only do we need to save all the townspeople from one another, but also we have to take down an evil corporation. Couldn't I have just one month when my biggest problem was being stressed about a math test?"

I turned to Charlie. "Earlier today, you said you had a plan."

He groaned. "I wanted us to sneak into Veratrum and try to find a way to disable their systems, forever. But this changes things. If they're backed up by a powerful company, I don't know what we can do."

"I still think we need to go," Marcus said. "We need to meet our enemy face-to-face."

"How would we even get there?" Willa asked. "It's on the outskirts of town. If we tried to walk, we'd spend all day fighting off zombies."

Charlie motioned to his brother. "My idea was that Jason would drive."

"Huh?" Jason said through a muffled full mouth. "But I don't have my license."

"It's the zombie apocalypse," Willa said. "There are no rules. Plus, it's not like there will be a ton of other cars on the road to deal with."

Jason thought for a moment, then shrugged. "Sure, why not?"

My heart fluttered in my chest, both with nerves and hope. Going to Veratrum headquarters was worth a try. It was better than sitting back and allowing them to put our town in danger again and again.

I clapped my hands together. "Then it's decided. Tomorrow, while our gamer army is doing their best to cure the town one zombie at a time, we're going to crash Veratrum headquarters and make sure this never happens again."

Charlie stood, his chair scraping against the floor. He raised his glass of water up in a toast. "Tonight, we sleep. And tomorrow, the nerds rise."

18

I opened my eyes, and for a few wonderful moments I forgot that our town had become a land of the undead. As my brain whirred to life, I tried to remember what day it was. Did I have school? Had I finished all my homework? And then, after those few blissful seconds, it all came back in a rush. Oh, yeah. We were zombie town. I heaved a sigh and swung my legs over the side of the bed.

But maybe today that would all change, and we could stop Veratrum forever.

I stretched and padded into the bathroom to splash

cold water on my face. I dressed for comfort in jeans and a hoodie, then headed downstairs. Willa and the boys were eating cereal around the kitchen table.

Charlie poked his head up. "Ready for our big day?"

"As ready as I'll ever be," I said, grabbing a bowl and filling it.

Marcus slid a printed photo across the table of a young guy with slicked-back blond hair and a tie as crooked as his fake smile.

The corners of my mouth automatically turned down. "Who's that?"

"Veratrum's CEO, Preston Frick."

I did a double take. "What is he, twelve?"

"He's twenty-four," Marcus said, "which is basically twelve in CEO years."

Charlie pointed at the picture. "If we see him at Veratrum, he's the guy to cure first. So we can get some answers out of that smug face."

Willa stood and started clearing empty bowls. "Has anyone heard from our gamer army?"

I chewed through a bite of cereal. "Vanya texted and said her parents and the diner's customers have all awakened and agreed to help. They're focusing on the stores on Main Street."

"The lax bros and football dudes are taking the south fields and the high school," Jason said.

Charlie scrolled through his texts. "Isaac, Andy, and a couple of others checked in. They're awake and human again. They've already started curing, all around town."

Good, I thought. So even if our visit to Veratrum turned up nothing, at least some progress would be made. I finished my cereal and chugged some orange juice.

Charlie hefted a backpack onto the table. "I packed all our phone chargers in case we need them. I have a pair of binoculars. A bunch of random stuff we may or may not need." He paused. "Jason, did you get that thing?"

"Yep." Jason passed Charlie something small, tightly wrapped in a paper bag.

"What's that?" Willa asked.

"You'll see." Charlie smiled secretively. "Okay, let's hit the road."

We headed outside to Charlie's driveway, where his mom's SUV sat waiting. Charlie dangled the keys in front of Jason, who reluctantly grabbed them.

"I don't know about this," Jason said.

Charlie patted him on the shoulder. "You'll do fine."

Willa agreed. "You're as big as an adult. You've driven go-karts before, right? How hard could it be?"

Apparently driving could be very hard. Or so we learned after Jason took out two mailboxes, several hedges, and three flowering bushes. I figured he'd get the hang of it after a while, but it had been five minutes and he still couldn't go straight down a wide road with nothing in his way.

"Don't overcompensate when you start to veer off!" Charlie yelled.

"Keep the wheel straight!" Marcus said.

Willa groaned. "I feel like I'm inside a pinball machine. And I'm the ball."

Jason raised his fist in the air. "You guys are the ones who made me do this!"

"Both hands on the wheel!" we all screamed.

We reached the outskirts of town where no one lived. There were only businesses, warehouses, and a couple of industrial buildings.

Marcus, who was sitting next to me in the middle row, slid a little closer. "When this is all over and we go back to school, you're going to check out that game I created, right?"

Really? That was what he was thinking about right now? "Yeah, sure," I said, watching out the window as a mailman zombie lurched across someone's front lawn.

Finally, with a screech and a sudden stop that made me silently thank the inventor of seatbelts, we reached Veratrum headquarters. The short, two-story brick building and its surrounding parking lot was enclosed by a chain-link fence. The gate was closed—not locked, just latched—but a couple of hastily abandoned cars blocked the entrance.

"Looks like the SUV stops here," Jason said.

Which normally wouldn't be a problem. We could just unlatch the gate and walk through the parking lot and up to the building.

If the place wasn't surrounded by zombies.

The chain-link fence was confining dozens of undead employees to the parking lot. They staggered around with their creepy gray eyes, bouncing off cars and one another, randomly grunting and groaning.

Charlie unzipped his backpack and took out the binoculars. He raised them to his eyes and peered through the windows of the office building. "There are a ton of zombies inside, too. Mostly on the first floor."

We groaned as if we were the ones who were infected. Charlie passed the binoculars around so we could all take a look.

Then Charlie released his seat belt and said, "You guys ready?"

"What?" Willa blurted. "How in the world are we going to get to the building?"

"And even if we get through the lot safely," I said, "how would we get inside? The zombies are clustered toward the glass front doors."

"Same answer for both." Charlie reached into his backpack with a smile. "Create a distraction."

He took out that small brown paper bag Jason had given him earlier and pulled something out of it. My eyes widened as I saw the label.

Willa gasped. "Are those firecrackers?"

"I prefer to call them zombie catnip," Charlie said. "We know the zombies are attracted to noise. This, and Jason's accurate arm, will ensure that the zombies go where we want them to."

Marcus pointed through the windshield. "How

about the far left side of the building? The zombies in the parking lot will gravitate there, away from the gate. And the zombies inside will go toward the west side windows, giving us a clear path through the front door."

"That's perfect," Charlie said, handing the small bundle to Jason.

Jason ripped open the thin red outer paper to reveal a package of small firecrackers. They looked like miniature sticks of dynamite or scary birthday candles.

"The wicks are tied together," Jason said, "so I'll light one and they'll all go off." He lifted them up in his fist and mimed throwing. "One problem, though. They're too light. Even at my hardest throw, they'll only go twenty feet."

Charlie scratched his chin. "We'll need to increase the mass so you can get a better distance." He fished around in his backpack and held up a roll of duct tape. "How about we find the perfect rock and tape it to the package?"

Jason nodded. "That'll work!"

"Okay," I said. "Let's get out. Try and be as quiet as possible."

We slid out of the SUV and hid behind it, hoping not to attract any zombie attention. Marcus found a good-size rock, and Charlie wound the duct tape around the entire package.

Willa had been peering through the binoculars. "Okay, guys. Once the zombie horde heads west, we unlatch the gate. The clearest path looks like it's straight through between the red compact and the silver convertible. Keep yourselves huddled down as you run, and use the parked cars as cover."

We all nodded.

Charlie placed the firecracker-and-rock bundle in Jason's hand. "Now can you reach the left side of the building?"

Jason flexed his arm, showing off his bicep. "What do you think?"

Charlie just shook his head. He pulled out a book of matches and lit one. "Let's do this."

A series of pops and sparks flew up from the ground as the firecrackers landed on the far left side of the building. A small plume of smoke followed. And so did the zombies.

We unlatched the gate and gingerly made our way into the parking lot. It took a minute for all of the zombies to realize something fun was going on at the end of the lot. Once they cleared out, we bolted for the front door of the building.

Charlie cupped his hands around his eyes and peered through the glass doors. "They're all clumped over by the west side windows," he whispered. "Just as planned. Be quiet, just in case."

We eased the door open and tiptoed over the threshold, careful not to let the door slam behind us. A black sign with tiny white letters hung on the entryway wall, detailing where the departments were located. My eyes scanned down the list—Accounting, Marketing, Development, Office of the CEO.

"Boom," I said. "Preston Frick is in office 201, second floor. Let's head there. Maybe we'll find some answers in his files."

"It looks like the staircase is in the center of the building," Charlie said, pointing into the distance.

We inched down the main hallway. The rug was an ugly spotted brown, but it muffled our footsteps. The building was like a corn maze, except with tall, gray cubicle walls instead of corn. Windows lined the perimeter and large offices and conference rooms took up the corners.

An undead groan came from behind a closed office door as we passed. Fluorescent lights flickered in the ceiling. Signs of struggle littered the floor from when the first employees started to change—a knocked-over chair, a broken coffee mug, a random stapler that perhaps someone had tried to use as a weapon.

I was glad the zombies had all bolted for the windows when the firecrackers went off, because passing each cubicle would have been terrifying if there was a possible zombie in each one. Instead of worrying about that, I focused on moving forward as quickly as I could, hunching over so my head wouldn't appear above a cubicle wall.

Until a hand lashed out from a cubicle opening and wrapped around my ankle.

I gasped, too loudly, and fell to the carpet.

Marcus was at my side immediately, pulling the zombie's fingers back until my ankle was free. "Don't worry," he whispered. "He's stuck."

The zombie's tie was caught on a coat hook that had been bolted into the cube wall, and his empty zombie brain hadn't figured out a way to free himself. The cubicle nameplate said Chris Edwards—Accountant. He'd probably been stuck like that for days, since the zombie apocalypse began.

Charlie snickered. "Talk about being chained to your desk."

Willa rolled her eyes at his joke but simultaneously smiled.

"Uh-oh," Jason said, peeking over the cubicle wall.

I hopped to my feet and took a quick look. The undead accountant wouldn't be a problem. But a couple of his zombie co-workers who'd heard my loud gasp and left the window to come this way were something to be concerned about.

"I think it's time to stop going at half-speed hunched over and just full-speed run for it," I said.

We all wordlessly agreed and took off. I risked a glance over my shoulder. A couple more zombies had joined the first two. The crowd was beginning to lose interest in the firecrackers now that the smoke cleared.

"We have to get up the stairs quickly," I said. There were still zombies on the second floor, but from what we'd seen through the binoculars, there weren't as many. Which sounded fantastic right about now.

Marcus skidded to a stop in front of the metal stairwell door. He wrapped his hand around the knob. "As soon as I pull this open, run in."

Because I was the one in front, I said, "Okay, go!"

He yanked open the door.

"*RARGH!*" A young woman with purple hair and really cool ankle boots reached her zombified hands out toward my face.

Startled, I grabbed her shoulders by instinct and twirled her around like we were dancing.

"Art Department is that way!" I yelled and gave her a push.

Everyone else had hustled into the stairwell. They pulled me in to join them and Marcus slammed the door shut, closing the cool zombie out. (Hey, she may have been undead, but I could still appreciate her style.)

"Any other surprises?" I asked, one hand on my rapidly beating heart.

Jason looked up the flight of stairs and gave us the all clear. "She was the only one."

We took a moment to catch our breath and dragged ourselves slowly up the staircase. There was a matching gray metal door on the second floor. I almost didn't want to open it. The stairwell was safe and zombie-free. But we'd come here for a reason, and procrastinating wasn't going to make things go any more smoothly. We just had to face whatever was waiting on the other side.

"There aren't as many up here," Charlie said. "We don't have to hide. We can take them on and cure them."

We all readied our phones. I took a deep breath and pushed the door open.

The smell hit us first. It was like someone had made chili in the microwave and then let it sit on the counter for three days. The first zombie we encountered had been hanging around the copy machine. He wore a crooked tie and one shoe.

We lined up four across and cured him in record time. The man blinked quickly and didn't even ask any questions before he dropped to the rug for his big nap.

Two women in stylish blazers were next. We tried to be stealthy and quiet, not attracting too much attention as we tossed our cures. Jason helped them into a nearby office, where they both quickly slumped into cushy desk chairs and closed their eyes.

"You guys," Willa whispered. "Here it is."

She'd stopped in front of a closed door. The Office of Preston Frick, CEO.

Charlie reached out hesitantly toward the knob. "Ready to cure if he's in there all zombified?"

In response, we held up our phones.

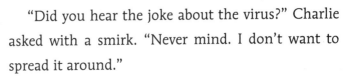

"Did you hear the joke about the virus?" Charlie asked with a smirk. "Never mind. I don't want to spread it around."

I let out a small groan. *Now, Charlie? Really?*

He turned the knob and pushed the door in.

The office was strangely furnished. It contained a giant mahogany desk that was too big for the room. Photos of yachts and Preston with various D-level celebrities hung in tacky gold frames on the walls.

"There are no filing cabinets," Willa said. "I thought we needed to go through his files."

"Everything's probably on his computer," I said, pointing to the sleek laptop that lay open on his desk. I could hear the fan whirring inside, so it was already on. But that was weird; a battery couldn't last that long.

I inched around the side of the desk. If the laptop was still on that meant that he'd been in here recently. I pulled back his desk chair and—

"*AHHHH!*" A screaming man came scrambling out from under the desk, waving a gold letter opener in front of his face like he was going to attack me with it. And when I realized who it was, he was lucky I didn't attack *him.*

20

W hoa, whoa," I said, holding my hands out in front of me. "We're human."

Preston Frick's eyes were wild with panic as he gazed at each of us in turn. He didn't look much like the picture I'd seen this morning, but it was him. That slicked back hair forked out in all directions. And his smug expression had been replaced by fear.

"You—you're children," he stammered, putting the letter opener down on his desk.

The CEO of Veratrum Games had been hiding in his office, probably taking a nap under his desk. No wonder he was startled at first. But now that he knew we were only kids and not zombies who'd figured out how to open a door, he shook off his fear and straightened his red tie.

"What are you doing here?" he snapped.

I jutted my chin out. "We're here to talk to you. We know Veratrum is responsible for the zombie outbreak."

"And the aliens," Willa added.

"And the monsters," Marcus said.

Charlie stepped right up to his face. "So you're going to reverse it. Now. Make everyone human again."

Preston laughed at us. Actually laughed. "Or what? What could *you* possibly do to *me*?"

I put my hands on my hips. "We found a way through a swarm of zombies in the parking lot, survived a horde of them lumbering around the building, and made it all the way up here to your fancy office where *you* were hiding under your desk. So maybe, just maybe, we could find a way to lure a couple of zombies in here and lock them in with you."

His eyes widened for a moment, then he looked down at his desk. "I can't fix it," he mumbled.

"What was that?" Charlie asked.

Preston looked back up at us with something like remorse in his eyes. "I tried. But rewriting the code didn't help. The only way to turn them human again is to play the game and cure them one by one. But there are too many . . ." His voice drifted off as a thought occurred to him. He plastered on a fake smile. "Now, with you kids here, we could make a team, right? You seem to really have a handle on this. You can go first and clear a path. I'll follow and—"

Jason puffed out his chest. "You want to use a group of kids as human shields? That's where you're going with this?"

"No, of course not," he said too quickly.

Willa clucked her tongue in disapproval. "Then what did you mean when you said 'you can go first and clear a path'?"

Preston gazed down at his hands, which had started to tremble. "I've been stuck in here for days."

"And we've been out on the streets curing zombies *you* made," Marcus said.

Preston lifted his hands in the air. "I can't fix it. I tried. So what else do you want me to do?"

I pulled the guest chair from the corner of the office and settled myself in. "How about you tell us the truth? The whole story. Why you created these games that weren't games. Why you unleashed these disasters on Wolcott."

He immediately got defensive. "It's wasn't—"

But Marcus cut in. "We know about your big contract. We know more than you think."

Preston's eyes shifted around nervously.

"We're all stuck here," Charlie said. "You might as well come clean."

"It might feel good to unload your conscience," Willa said, "if you have one."

Preston's chest rose and fell as he took a big breath. He lowered himself down to his chair. "They *were* real games, everywhere else in the world. The variations were only in the games downloaded here in town."

"Variations," I repeated with disgust. He said it like he'd offered the people of Wolcott a new flavor of Popsicle rather than put their lives in danger. Anger leaked into my voice. "So everyone else in the world got normal games and we got . . . variations."

"I needed a testing ground." He tapped his fingers nervously on the arms of the chair. "It only made sense to do it in the town where we're headquartered."

"You know what would have made better sense?" Willa snapped. "Not doing it at all!"

He shook his head sadly. The bags under his eyes seemed to sag, and he looked much older than twenty-four. "You kids would never understand."

"Try us," Charlie said. "Tell us why."

Preston stood up from his chair and began to pace around the office. "My father gave me a million dollars to start this company."

"Rough life," Marcus said. "The struggle is real."

Preston ignored him and continued. "I blew through his initial investment. I mismanaged everything. But I couldn't go crawling back to him asking for more. I couldn't shut down the company and admit that I'd failed!"

"Yeah, destroying an entire town is a great way to save face," I said.

"That wasn't supposed to happen!" He dragged his hands through his gelled hair, making it stick straight up. "I accepted the contract because I needed the money. I never thought anything bad would happen."

"What was the contract for, then?" Marcus asked.

"The variation on *Monsters Unleashed* was to see if we could get video game characters to affect the real world. They wanted to see if, down the line, they could create video game armies and sell those to governments. Something like that could save human lives! So I ran a small test in town with cute monsters."

"Cute?" Charlie snapped. "A SpiderFang nearly killed me!"

Preston waved his hand dismissively. "I never thought it would work. I thought I'd just take the money and move forward with my regular games."

And maybe, if we hadn't been playing around with that machine in Grandpa Tepper's attic, it *wouldn't* have worked. The old machine belonged to an ex-Veratrum employee and was the catalyst that kicked it all off. But I wasn't going to volunteer that information to Mr. Evil Genius here so he could figure out why it happened and create more disasters with it.

"What about *Alien Invasion?*" I asked. "What secret test was in there?"

"We were experimenting with teleportation, with a goal of quickly moving supplies or eventually people from one place to another. But the test never worked. I heard rumors that actual aliens got teleported here to town, but I never saw any. I even sent a guy to do surveillance and he said it was a bust."

The test *did* work. But only in combination with an astrophysicist's work-in-progress alien-contacting machine at the observatory. And that "guy" followed us around in a white van with a fake plumbing logo on the side. Like we didn't know how to check business names online to see if they were real.

Preston may have thought he had a handle on his games, but he didn't count on how they would interact with outside software and hardware. It was like the time my phone downloaded an update and my unrelated weather app started to insist I was in India. He could never have predicted or tested for me to be using a game next to an outdated Veratrum device or the machine at the observatory. He thought he was in control, but he wasn't.

"And *Zombie Town?*" Willa asked.

Preston gazed at the floor. "This is when I really

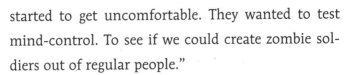

started to get uncomfortable. They wanted to test mind-control. To see if we could create zombie soldiers out of regular people."

"And even though you were 'uncomfortable,' you did it anyway," Willa sneered. "This is all your fault."

Preston sat back down heavily in his chair. "It wasn't supposed to be like this. The test went off too soon."

I leaned forward. "Excuse me?"

"I signed the contract to keep my company afloat. I figured I could keep everything safe here in town. But after the monsters got unleashed, I knew this was the wrong path. I told them I was out. They'd have to find another developer to work with. But they wouldn't release me from the contract. They wouldn't let me stop. They said they'd leak what happened to the press. I'd get blamed. My company would be shut down. My career would be over."

"So you made 'variations' on two more games," I prodded.

"I didn't see any way out. I couldn't tell my father what I'd gotten involved in."

My hands clenched into fists. I couldn't believe

this was all because of some selfish dweeb and his daddy issues.

He continued, "I knew the *Zombie Town* code wasn't ready, but they said I had to launch the test right away."

"Why rush it?" Charlie asked.

Preston groaned in frustration. "We had a whistleblower. I don't know who, but one of my employees was feeding information to the cops."

Detective Palamidis's appointment. It all made sense now.

"The test didn't go well," Preston said as a moaning zombie shuffled past the office. "Obviously. But I figured things would course-correct like they did before. I waited in here. But nothing is happening."

I held a finger up. "Um, what do you mean 'course-correct'?"

Preston shrugged. "Monsters got unleashed into town and then disappeared. Aliens might have been here, but I never saw them; so if they were, they disappeared, too. I figured the zombies would also go that way."

Willa spoke through gritted teeth. "You think the

monsters and aliens magically went away? It. Was. Us. We saved the town."

"You kids?" He gave a dismissive snort. "How?"

"We caught every single monster," I said. "One by one. A SpiderFang nearly ate Charlie!"

Charlie shuddered at the memory and added, "And we captured all of the aliens and transported them back home after a code rewrite."

Preston gawked at him. *"You're* the one who reversed that line of code in *Alien Invasion?"*

"They did it," Charlie said, pointing to Marcus and me.

"You're, what, middle school kids?" he asked, his voice tinged with disbelief.

Marcus shrugged. "Yeah. And we've spent the last few days curing as many zombies as we could while you were hiding in your office."

Preston stared blankly for a moment, then his face crumbled. "It should be you," he said, his voice trembling, "running a company like this. Not me."

Marcus and I glanced at each other and smiled.

"Maybe someday," I said. *Gamer Squad* would be a great name for a game development company.

"But flattering us isn't going to get you anywhere right now."

Charlie crossed his arms in front of his chest. "We want you to promise, if we make it out of this one alive, that it's the last mess you create. Veratrum Games is shut down, immediately and forever."

I softened my voice. "I know it's going to feel bad, telling your father that your company is gone. But you have to do the right thing, even if it's uncomfortable."

Preston hunched his shoulders. "You're right. I can't go on like this. It's gone too far this time."

"You promise Veratrum is done? No more shady contracts?" Willa asked.

He nodded. "That company won't even want to work with me anymore after this disaster. It's over."

I exhaled loudly. I almost couldn't believe it. We'd meticulously crafted a plan and it had all worked. Our gamer army was out curing zombies. We'd stopped Veratrum forever. Now we just had to get out of here, and we could join our army and cure zombies until every last person in Wolcott was human again. We could do it. Hope rose in me like an old friend I hadn't spent time with in a while.

My phone buzzed in my pocket. Charlie's started chirping. Then Willa's, Marcus's, and even Jason's phone. People were trying to reach us all at once.

I slid my phone out of my pocket and scrolled through the panicked incoming texts. "Something's wrong," I said. "All the zombies are at the middle school. All at once."

"Our gamer army is overwhelmed," Charlie said, his voice worried. "Why would the zombies suddenly all go to one place?"

"Ohhhhhh," Preston said slowly.

I gritted my teeth. "What?"

He let out a shaky breath. "There was another line of code in *Zombie Town* that the buyer requested. They wanted the zombies to be able to assemble."

Charlie and I shared a look. "What does that mean?" I asked.

"It's a built-in feature that forces the zombies to assemble in one place. To attack an enemy target, let's say. Rather than having the zombies mindlessly wander, they all descend upon the target at once."

"And you didn't think that was important information for us to have after we told you we've built up a gamer army?" Willa screeched. "Our army is the enemy target!"

Preston raised his hands into the air. "I didn't think it would happen. The code was in there, but it wasn't finished. I didn't fill in the trigger variable so I figured it wouldn't work."

"You figured," I repeated, seething. "And this is why you shouldn't be making games. You push out unfinished code without testing and are *shocked* when something unexpected happens."

"They made me run it before I was ready!" he yelled.

"Oh, sure, it's all *their* fault," I snapped back.

"Guys," Marcus said. "Arguing about it isn't helping our gamer army."

"He's right," I said, standing. "We have to go help them. Now!"

Charlie glanced at the office door. "Quick question. How do we get out?"

21

Marcus peered through the small window beside the office door. "I see only a few zombies milling about on this floor. We could take them."

Willa chewed on her thumbnail. "Yeah, but there are a lot more downstairs. Plus the parking lot."

Preston's forehead scrunched up. "How *did* you manage to get through all of the zombies to get up here?"

"A little firecracker distraction," Jason explained. "But we don't have any more."

Charlie was suspiciously quiet. He paced the room, checking out every nook and cranny with his thinking face on.

I sidled up next to him. "Any ideas?"

"Just because the firecrackers are gone, that doesn't mean we can't find another distraction." He stopped at Preston's desk and pointed at a small box. "What's this?"

"It's an intercom," Preston said. "I can use it to talk to people in conference rooms."

"So you speak into this box and the voice comes out in the conference room?" Charlie asked. "Which one?"

"Whichever one I want," Preston answered. "Even all of them."

My heart sped up. We'd passed a couple of conference rooms on our way that had their doors open. I wondered . . . "How loud can you make it?"

Preston shrugged. "I don't make it a point to yell at my employees, but I suppose I could be really loud if I tried."

Charlie and I shared a look. Willa, Marcus, and Jason moved closer.

"This is how we escape," I said. "We lure the zombies into conference rooms and then walk right out the east side door. The parking lot zombies will still mostly be around the west side of the building."

"One problem," Charlie said. "Someone would have to stay behind to keep talking into the intercom."

I closed my eyes. Of course. I didn't think of that.

"I'll do it," Preston said.

My eyes snapped open. "What?"

He nodded quickly like he was convincing himself. "You kids go. I owe you at least this much."

"Are you sure?" Marcus said. "We can't have you chickening out halfway through and getting us all zombified."

Preston stuck his chin out confidently. "Yes, I'm sure."

"Once we help our gamer army with the horde, we'll send some people back for you," I promised.

"Sure," he said, but almost like he didn't believe it. Like he didn't think we'd survive.

"We have to go now," Charlie said, looking at his phone. "They need us."

App of the Living Dead

"Don't worry," Preston said. "I can talk for a *long* time."

I believed it.

He took a deep breath and pressed the button on the intercom. Then he yelled at the top of his lungs, "Good day, zombies!"

I cringed and Willa put her hands over her ears. Preston was right. He *could* get loud.

He continued at a frenzied pitch. "Today, in your nearest conference room, we have a sale on brains! Yummy, yummy brains! Don't you want some! You have no idea what I'm saying so I'm just going to yell anything! I'M NOT AFRAID OF YOU, DAD! I'M DOING THE RIGHT THING NOW!"

While Preston began his own personal therapy session with the intercom, we peeked out the office door. The zombies on this floor seemed to be in a big rush to get to the far corner, where an open door led to a suddenly noisy conference room. It was working!

We slipped out of the office and strode down the hall to the stairwell. At least we already knew that was clear. Jason pulled open the gray metal door and we hustled inside.

"One floor done," Charlie said.

"Yeah, the easy floor," Willa said worriedly.

In a single-file line, we raced down the steps, then huddled around the door to the first floor. I reached a hand out toward the cool metal. Anything could be waiting on the other side. That cool zombie chick. Or *all* the first-floor zombies, gathered around like hungry dogs at dinnertime. I hoped the intercoms were working down here, too. I threw my weight against the door, and we emptied out into the hall.

Nothing.

Preston's voice carried from a nearby conference room. "Remember, zombies, this sale on brains is today only! Fifty percent off! Left brain, right brain, eat your favorite!"

"I think he's losing it," Willa whispered.

"As long as it works," I said.

We ducked for cover inside a nearby cubicle. Marcus peeked his head over the top to take a look.

"One or two stragglers are still making their way toward the conference room," he said, "but all the others are already inside looking for the source of the noise."

"Do we have a clear path to the east side exit?" Charlie asked.

Marcus nodded. "Just try to keep your heads lower than the cube walls."

We hurried toward the door, heads down, mouths shut. So far, all the zombies were attracted to Preston's voice. We needed to not make any sound that would lure them toward us.

When we reached the east side exit, Charlie pushed the door open and held it until we were all out. I held up my hand against the bright sunlight until my eyes adjusted. The zombies had moved on from the firecracker distraction and were clamoring at the fence on the west side. They were trying to get to the school. That assemble code did one good thing. It gave us a clear path back to the car.

Jason even drove better on the way to the middle school. He only hit one mailbox. I guess practice does help.

But when he slammed on the brakes at the entrance to the school lot, we all gasped at the sight before us. It was even worse than I'd imagined. Our gamer army was surrounded by more zombies than I could count.

And even more zombies were pouring in—from the street, the woods, the spaces between houses.

The parking lot looked as packed as a football tailgate party. There were so many zombies that they were even tripping on one another and falling into zombie pile-ons, like a strange undead version of wrestling.

It was an actual, living nightmare.

And we *had* to go help them.

The five of us hopped out of the SUV and immediately started tossing cures. Some of our gamer army people were still standing, fighting in the middle of the growing pack. But many of them had been turned back into zombies already.

It was chaos. Three zombies came at me. Marcus pushed one away while I tossed cures at the other two. But a fourth came up behind me, grabbing my shoulder. I twisted and turned. Willa and Charlie tossed cures to save me. Somewhere in the scrum, I got hit in the nose with a flying elbow. My eyes watered, making everything blurry.

"We need a strategy," Jason said.

"He's right," Charlie called out. "Fan out in a line. Don't move forward. Let the zombies come toward us and cure them one at a time. If everyone stays focused and clears the zombies in front of them, this may work."

It was a good plan. Most of the undead were huddled toward the center, surrounding our gamer army and closing in fast. If we busted into that crowd, we'd get overwhelmed just like they were. This way, we could pick them off one by one from the outside, dwindling their numbers, like a shark does to a school of fish.

"Remember," Charlie yelled. "No distractions. Focus on the zombies right in front of you."

I checked the battery life on my phone. Over 50 percent. I was in good shape. A zombie lumbered toward me, a guy about my dad's age, wearing jeans and a flannel shirt. I hit him square in the head with my first shot. He blinked a few times and immediately fell to the ground. He didn't even have time to get confused before he took his big nap.

As long as the zombies kept coming little by little like this, we'd be in good shape. I cured another zombie, then took a moment to let my eyes wander and check out the status of our gamer army who were struggling in the middle of the big horde.

But I saw something else instead.

The ground seemed to tilt and sway under my feet. My parents were here. They were at the edge of the big zombie horde, trying to get at my friends in the middle. At the sight of their familiar faces, even if they were dirty and zombified, my heart rose up into my throat. I'd missed them so much the last few days. And now that longing—to hug them, to talk to them—was so strong that it almost hurt.

"Bex!" Willa said, snapping me out of it. "Your zombie is getting a little close."

"Oh, right." I launched a cure, then a second. The woman in her cute cloud pajamas briefly looked around, said, "What in the world?" and fell to the ground beside the others.

"My parents are here," I said to Willa.

"Cool. We'll get to them eventually." She frowned as she missed a shot, then refocused on her phone to throw another.

I didn't want to wait, though. I didn't want to get to them eventually. I wanted to cure them now. I *needed* to cure them now.

"Just get my zombies, too, while I take care of this," I said.

"What?" Willa looked at me. "No! Stick to the plan."

"It will only take a minute," I argued. "I'll come

right back. Just cure your zombies and mine for a second."

I broke away from our line and approached the outskirts of the big group.

"Mom? Dad?" My voice trembled. My parents didn't turn to look at me, though. Their attention—and that of the other zombies—was fully on the dwindling gamer army in the middle. Mostly because of their panicked screams.

"I'm going to cure you!" I yelled, aiming my phone.

I tossed a cure at the back of my mom's head. It bounced off my dad's shoulder, angering him, and he swatted at it like a mosquito.

"Bex!" Charlie yelled. "What are you doing?"

"Just give me a second!" I called back.

My dad's attention got pulled from the action in front of him, and he turned around and headed toward me.

"Um, okay, hi." I stopped trying to cure my mom, who had been frustratingly swaying back and forth, missing each of my tosses, and focused on my dad. I frantically sent three cures in a row, all the while stepping backward as he got closer.

Finally, I landed one, square in the center of his forehead.

He shook his head and blinked quickly. He only had time to say, "Bex?" before he fell to the ground.

But then dread filled me as I looked behind him. My mom was heading this way, too. And others from the edge of the group had noticed me. It wasn't just singular zombies breaking off from the group now. The horde was splitting in two.

"Need a little help here!" Marcus called out.

"I have too many!" Willa yelled.

Cries of pain and panic were all around me. Almost all of the gamer army had been bitten and they were turning back. So the zombies were now headed toward us . . . the last humans in the lot.

"Retreat!" Charlie yelled as he ducked from a lunging zombie. "We need to get into the school."

Willa shrieked at the top of her lungs as a little kid zombie bit her ankle.

"No!" I cried.

A group of football-jersey wearing zombies reached for Charlie. Jason jumped in the way, sacrificing himself. He attempted to climb out of the fray, only to be dragged back down.

I reeled backward, my eyes scanning the lot. There was one clear path to the school, between two abandoned buses. I could make it, but Charlie and Marcus were too far behind.

"Go!" Charlie ordered. "Get inside. Get safe. Figure out a new plan."

I refused to give up, launching cure after cure, but it wasn't fast enough. The zombies were turning faster than they were being cured. And the ones who were cured were sleeping it off rather than helping.

I heard Charlie cry out and turned in time to see Jason chomp down on his shoulder. Bitten by his own brother. Not for the first time—if I remembered the kindergarten incident correctly—but the consequences of this bite were more severe. I turned my head, unable to watch my best friend change into a member of the undead.

Marcus climbed on the roof of a car, surrounded by zombies grabbing at his legs. "Go, Bex!"

My throat clenched in panic. It was hard to get deep breaths.

"I'm not leaving you!" I cried.

"You have to! You're the last of us. If you turn, too, the town is toast!"

I staggered to the side, heading down the clear path between the buses.

"Remember to look at the big picture," Marcus called. "You'll figure something out."

I ran blindly, imagining zombie hands grabbing for my arms and legs. I rushed through the front doors of the school and closed them quickly behind me. Then I peered out the window at the car where Marcus had stood. It was empty. He was down with the others.

I was the only one left.

scanned the main hall. It seemed empty. I just had to get to a room where I could sit, collect my thoughts, and figure out a plan. I willed my feet to move forward.

Mr. Durr groaned from behind the closed door of a classroom. He'd been contained by someone at some point, but that didn't mean other zombies weren't roaming the halls. I poked my head into the computer lab. It was empty. This would be as good a place as any to rest.

I closed the door and slid down the wall to the floor, pulling my knees up to my chest. I couldn't believe this happened. Everything had gone so wrong. If only I hadn't tried to cure my parents. If only we'd gotten to our gamer army earlier. Charlie and Marcus had seemed confident that I'd come up with another plan, but I felt hopeless. I had no other ideas. No matter how hard I tried to think of one.

I gazed around the room looking for anything. A forgotten notebook lay on the floor. A framed photo of our entire class hung on the wall. I remembered when we posed for it, the first day of school. Charlie had pushed through the crowd to make sure he was standing next to me. A bunch of kids in the back had made bunny ears with their fingers, and the photographer made us start over. I looked away. I didn't want to see all the happy, excited faces, knowing how many of them were zombified right now.

The swirling screensaver on one of the computer terminals caught my eye. It was the one Marcus had wanted to show me his new project on before we had an emergency dismissal from school. That seemed like three years ago, not three days.

I pulled myself up to standing and dusted off my

jeans. With a quick jiggle of the mouse, the screen-saver dissolved and a list of files appeared. In the chaos of dismissal, Marcus had forgotten to log out. The top file, FOR BEX, stared at me.

I wondered if it was wrong for me to open it without him. But, then again, he was currently staggering around the parking lot as a zombie. I had no idea how to fix the situation. We might not get out of this one. Marcus had been so excited to show me his new game. I was stuck in here anyway . . .

I double-clicked on the file.

Jingly, happy music began to play and a gray sidewalk appeared on the screen. A character who looked very much like Marcus walked to the middle of the scene. A huge smile broke out on my face. Then a second character—a girl in jeans and a T-shirt with freckles and frizzy hair pulled up into a ponytail—walked up to computer Marcus. My mouth dropped open. That was *me*. The graphics were a little glitchy, but that was clearly me.

A thought bubble appeared above Marcus's head with the words **HI, BEX.** Underneath was the call to action, **click to continue**. Stifling a giggle, I reached out and clicked the mouse.

HI, MARCUS! my character said.

I clicked to continue again.

I HAVE SOMETHING TO ASK YOU, Computer Marcus said.

My shaking hand clicked to continue again.

OKAY, Computer Bex replied.

Marcus's character suddenly had a bunch of flowers in his hand. They came out of nowhere—total plot hole—but I clicked to go on.

WILL YOU GO TO THE DANCE WITH ME? Computer Marcus asked.

And then a big box came up on the screen with a checkbox for **YES** and **NO**.

My heart soared. It wasn't a game Marcus wanted to show me, not really. It was an invitation. He must have spent hours creating this. He'd worked so hard.

Tears pricked my eyes as I selected **YES** and clicked.

The screen filled with hearts. Pink hearts, red hearts, small hearts, huge hearts. They flowed toward the middle of the screen from all corners. Then the game/invitation ended.

Willa was right. I still didn't know if *catastrophizing*

was a real word, but I'd definitely been assuming the worst about everything. Marcus hadn't asked me to the dance yet, so I thought he didn't like me at all. Meanwhile, he'd been working on the perfect invitation. And if I had been so wrong about that, maybe I was wrong about other things, too.

I was not this hopeless, pessimistic person I'd become. I was smart. I was tough. I never gave up. It had been a rough few months, but I'd been looking at things the wrong way. Instead of thinking about how it was my phone that had unleashed monsters into town, I should have focused on how it was my friends and I who had recaptured them. Instead of it being my fault that aliens were summoned here, it was our combined strength and smarts that figured out how to overcome Veratrum and send the aliens back home. And now, even at our lowest point, our town overwhelmed by zombies, I still stood. I survived.

And I was going to bring my friends back. Right now.

I started to pace in the computer lab. *Use your brain, Bex. Think. Like Marcus said, big picture.* I stared at the group photo on the wall. It was our entire class—together—the nerds and the jocks, the popular and the not-so-much, the gamers and non-gamers. In a rush, I realized my mistake.

In building our army, we focused on the gamers. We had to think bigger. There was a whole community out there who cared about Wolcott and the people in it. Surely, the majority of them could download a game and toss cures with a few instructions. I didn't need a *gamer* army. I needed the whole town. Anyone who wasn't a zombie. And I knew exactly how to reach them.

I sat down at the computer terminal and typed up a script. I reread it and gave it a few edits—changing references from zombie to "mind altering flu." It sounded less scary that way. Then I printed it out.

Creeping back into the hallway, I looked left and right to make sure I was alone. When I reached the classroom where I knew Mr. Durr was contained, I took a peek through the little window in the door. Predictably, Mr. Durr was at the large classroom window, staring at the chaos in the parking lot.

As quietly as possible, I turned the knob and inched open the door. Then I steeled myself, aimed my phone, and tossed a cure that landed right in the center of the back of Mr. Durr's head.

He turned around, confused, his eyes returning to their normal color.

I swooped in, grabbing him by the arm, and pulled him along with me to my final destination.

"What's going on?" he said slowly. "Where are we going? What's happening?"

"You were a zombie," I said, pulling him as I tried to speed-walk down the hall. "For, like, three days. I cured you but you're going to fall asleep soon. Possibly very soon. So we're in a hurry."

"Still . . . don't . . . understand."

He was getting heavier to pull, but I moved him forward with all my might. When we finally reached the office, I settled him into the chair behind Principal James's desk. His eyes widened as he saw the scene outside the window.

"They're—they're all—" He could only point a shaky finger at the zombies.

"It's okay," I said as soothingly as possible as I booted up the principal's computer. "We're going to get help."

I put the script into Mr. Durr's hands. "You need to log into the emergency autocall system. I can type up the email and maybe even leave the phone message. But I need you to log into the system."

Mr. Durr's eyes glazed over, and I jiggled his chair. "Stay with me!"

"Okay, okay." He pointed at an icon on the computer screen. "I've seen him do this before. Click on that."

The emergency autocall program opened. But there was a password required. I turned to Mr. Durr.

He shrugged. "I don't know his password."

I picked up the keyboard from Mr. James's desk and found a sticky note underneath: *grownups*. So predictable.

"Here you go," I said, handing the password to Mr. Durr. "Quickly, before you fall asleep."

He leaned over the keyboard and logged into the system. He showed the different options to me. "You can type up an email and send it here. You can select parents of students in the middle school only or any school in town."

"The whole town, definitely," I said. "And how about a phone call?"

He double clicked on an option. "I think I just speak into this mic here to record it, and then we send it off. I'm getting so sleepy though."

He blinked slowly as his eyes got heavy.

"You have to fight it!" I said, shaking his shoulder. "Only one more minute!"

I shoved the speech into his hands. "Read that in your most authoritative teacher voice. Then you can sleep."

Mr. Durr did his best, speaking into the microphone, telling parents in town what they needed to do. How to download the game and start playing. To congregate at the middle school. To tell everyone they knew to join them. He only started to slur at the end.

When he finished and we sent the recording off to ring in thousands of phones, I took his place in front of the computer and quickly typed up the exact same message in an email. Then we sent that. And I took a moment to breathe.

"Now what?" Mr. Durr asked, his eyes rolling up and refocusing.

"Now we wait," I said.

"Or we sleep," he mumbled as he slumped down in his chair.

I gave him a little pat on the shoulder, even though he wouldn't feel it. I knew it must have been hard to fight off sleep, but he'd done it. We'd sent out the message. Now we just had to hope they'd come.

I waited at the window, watching the zombies mill about, feeling more nervous with each minute that ticked by on the wall clock. Worried thoughts pushed their way into my head.

The system didn't work. No one got the call or email.

The message wasn't convincing enough.

No one will come.

But instead of indulging the thoughts, I pushed them away. I told that annoying voice that it was wrong. This *would* work. I knew it. I had faith in my town.

Then, from a nearby house, came a person holding a phone high. Then another came from the woods. And a car pulled up.

They came from all sides in all forms. Families in cars. Kids on bikes. Adults on foot. Some were confident, some scared. But they all held their phones up and *tried*. And before I knew it there were more of us than them. As the zombies started to sway and drop and sleep it off, my heart soared in my chest.

We'd enlisted the gamers while ignoring most everyone else. And in that mistake, I'd forgotten what I loved most about Wolcott. We were a community.

I ran out of the building and joined them—young and old, tall and short, gamer and not. Some were familiar faces and some I'd never seen before. But we all shared a love for our town and we wouldn't stop until it was saved.

We had started small, but more and more people showed up. We whittled the zombie horde down to only a few. When there was one last zombie left, a little boy threw the final cure.

"Ha!" he yelled. "I finally got one!"

With my heart in my throat and tears in my eyes, I searched the sleeping bodies until I found my parents. I settled in on the ground beside them, cradling their heads in my lap. I decided to stay with them until they woke up. And then we'd go home.

23

Charlie slapped the newspaper against my locker. It was Monday morning and everything was back to normal. Well, mostly. The cured had slept most of Friday. And the town needed most of Saturday and Sunday to clean up.

I glanced at the headlines of *The Wolcott Observer*.

RARE MIND-ALTERING FLU TEARS THROUGH TOWN.

"Ha!" I said. They used the term I'd put in my emergency message.

"Check out the story underneath that one," Charlie said.

My eyes scanned down.

VERATRUM GAMES OUT OF BUSINESS.

I skimmed the story quickly. There was talk around town that a game the company had created caused the flu epidemic, but anyone in a position to investigate it laughed at that idea. Most of the employees were getting snapped up by a rival game company headquartered in Runswick. But not the CEO. "I'm taking some time off," Preston Frick stated. "I'm going to travel and do some thinking about where I want to go from here."

"We did it," Charlie said.

I felt a swell of pride. "We sure did."

Veratrum wouldn't be unleashing disasters on our town anymore. We were safe.

But Charlie still looked nervous.

"What's up with you?" I asked.

He glanced around the hall like he was looking to

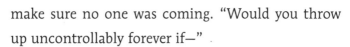
make sure no one was coming. "Would you throw up uncontrollably forever if—"

"If Willa became your girlfriend?" I guessed.

Charlie's eyes widened in shock. "How did you know?"

"I am your smartest friend. But I think even William Shakespaw had this mystery solved."

"So . . ." His voice trailed off, waiting for my answer.

It would definitely feel weird at first, to watch Charlie hold her hand or something like that. But he was my best friend and she was my second best. If this made them happy, then why not? I'd get used to it soon enough.

"I wouldn't puke *forever*," I said with a smirk. "Just once or twice like with a twenty-four-hour flu. Without the zombification."

"Really?" His eager eyes twinkled like I'd just mouthed the kindest words in the world.

"Really. Now go ask her to the Halloween Dance before someone way more cool and popular asks her."

Charlie punched me lightly in the arm, then ran off. And someone new walked up.

"Hey," Marcus said.

"Hey, yourself," I replied because I was totally cool like that with unique comebacks.

Marcus and I hadn't really had the chance to talk since Friday. After he slept it off, his parents had kept him at home, understandably wanting some together time. But now he had that nervous look in his eyes, just like Charlie had.

He scuffed his shoe back and forth against the floor. "I heard you and Charlie talking about the dance."

"Yeah, he's going to ask Willa."

Marcus's eyes snapped up to mine. "Oh! Good!" He let out a small, relieved breath, and I realized he'd been worried that Charlie had been asking *me*.

"Would you like to go?" I asked.

His mouth dropped open. "What?"

"Do you want to go to the dance together?"

His dreamy hazel eyes lit up. "Um, yeah. I mean, yes. I mean . . . I was going to ask you with this thing I made, but then the whole zombie thing happened."

I smirked. "Zombie apocalypses do tend to put a damper on things."

Marcus aimed a thumb at a poster on the wall

advertising the dance. "Should we go in costume or regular clothes?"

"Like what? A zombie? An alien? A monster?" I jokingly suggested. "I've seen enough of those for a lifetime. My vote's for regular clothes."

"Me, too," he said with a smile. "I like you just the way you are."